An Empire of Stones

A Shade of Vampire, Book 37

Bella Forrest

Also by Bella Forrest:

A SHADE OF DRAGON:

A Shade of Dragon 1

A Shade of Dragon 2

A Shade of Dragon 3

BEAUTIFUL MONSTER DUOLOGY:

Beautiful Monster 1

Beautiful Monster 2

A SHADE OF KIEV TRILOGY:

A Shade of Kiev 1

A Shade of Kiev 2

A Shade of Kiev 3

DETECTIVE ERIN BOND

(Adult mystery/thriller)

Bare Girl

Write, Edit, Kill

For an updated list of Bella's books, please visit her website:
www.bellaforrest.net

Join Bella's VIP email list and she'll personally send you an email reminder as soon as her next book is out! Visit here to sign up:
www.forrestbooks.com

Contents

THE "NEW GENERATION" NAMES LIST

- **Arwen:** (daughter of Corrine and Ibrahim - witch)
- **Benedict:** (son of Rose and Caleb - human)
- **Brock:** (son of Kiev and Mona – half warlock)
- **Grace:** (daughter of Ben and River – half fae and half human)
- **Hazel:** (daughter of Rose and Caleb – human)
- **Heath:** (son of Jeriad and Sylvia – half dragon and half human)
- **Ruby:** (daughter of Claudia and Yuri – human)
- **Victoria:** (daughter of Vivienne and Xavier – human)

ROSE

We had returned to The Shade as soon as we'd seen the air ambulance approaching. We'd ended up taking five of the less mindless, and more talkative, humans with us back to Meadow Hospital for the jinn and witches to heal, and to hopefully get some comprehensive answers out of them— though I wasn't holding out much hope. Even the best of the bunch were so far gone they couldn't even tell us their own names.

We'd left them in the care of Corrine and her team of nurses overnight, but waiting was proving difficult—we all desperately needed answers. As soon as we got back to the island, Caleb charged Benedict's dead phone, but it contained nothing helpful—the last message he'd sent was to Julian, asking him what assortment of games he'd be bringing along for the trip to Murkbeech.

We were unable to get any rest. At ten in the evening, Claudia and Yuri had joined us at our home, along with Ashley and Landis. We had spent the night speculating what kind of creature could have distorted the minds of humans so thoroughly. My mom had come over to join us, and seemed equally baffled—we'd told her what the young English boy had said, about dark hooded beings appearing in dreams and leaving them 'empty'.

We had gone around in circles till dawn, mostly waiting for a word from Corrine that we could visit the hospital and ask the humans more questions. Without them it was all just guesswork—and we had very little conclusive evidence to go on.

Eventually the group disbanded, and Caleb had gone off to speak via phone to the human hospital officials, who were as clueless as we were about what happened at the camp.

I found my mom sitting on the porch, overlooking the tops of the trees, deep in thought.

"What are you thinking?" I asked.

She took my hand, drawing me down to sit with her, and sighed. "I delayed telling you because you've got so much on your plate, but… it's your father and Ben. Sherus showed up on Ben's doorstep a few hours ago, requesting he and Dad travel to the fae realm for a meeting soon. Sherus didn't say why he needed them; I'm not sure of the reason for his sudden appearance."

Sherus. That ginger-haired fae who was responsible for giving my brother a living body. I felt quite stunned that he had visited after so long… and concerned. What did he want?

"You have no idea at all what he came for?" I asked.

"Sherus said that there's something coming—something that we should all be afraid of… he just doesn't know *what.* Or he does, and is keeping information from us."

"River must be worried," I murmured, thinking of my sister-in-law. She had almost lost Ben because of Sherus and the stupid deal he'd made with the ghouls to keep feeding them a fresh supply of ghosts.

My mom nodded. "Ben's at home with her now, trying to reassure her I think. They'll leave tomorrow."

"Well, I suppose there's no point in worrying till we know more," I muttered. I couldn't see any reason why Sherus would attempt to harm my father and brother.

"You're right," my mom replied, trying to be reassuring, but her paler-than-usual skin indicated just how deep her worries ran. "The priority is your children and Julian and Ruby…" She squeezed my hand. "I don't doubt that we'll find them, Rose. They take after you and Caleb—smart, resourceful and strong."

I hugged her, privately thinking that at least half of those qualities most definitely came from her. We didn't talk about the kids again, or Ben and my father, but quietly sat in silence—both turning over possibilities and outcomes in our head, desperately searching for solutions and impatient to know more.

The next morning, Caleb and I were anxiously looking through local police reports in Scotland and the rest of the British Isles to see if there had been any news of events similar to what happened in Murkbeech. Before we could find anything of interest, Corrine knocked on the kitchen window, beckoning us outside onto the veranda.

"One of the patients has started to make a bit more sense," she informed us. "Nothing much to go on, but you should come and hear what he has to say. Honestly, I've never heard anything quite like it," she added grimly.

She vanished us to the hospital, where we met up with Mona and Shayla, who'd apparently fetched Claudia, Yuri, Ashley and Landis.

Corrine led us into one of the rooms; the boy Caleb and I had spoken to on the island—the blond, British boy—was sitting up in bed, looking around the room in dull surprise. He focused on us as we entered, and once more his gaze zoomed in on mine. He furrowed his brow, as if he half recognized me, but couldn't quite place where he knew me from.

"Hazel?" he asked.

My heartbeat quickened as I walked slowly toward his bed, careful not to startle him.

"That's my daughter," I replied. "Do you know her?"

"I think I scared her," he said sadly. "But I don't know...I don't remember much."

"Can you tell us what you do remember?"

The others waited behind me, leaning in toward the boy, but careful not to crowd him. I glanced at Corrine and she gave me an encouraging nod.

The boy was silent for a moment, and then began to speak.

"I suppose first it was the camp organizers...I remember them being weird—nice one minute and then angry the next. Then people started getting headaches. We thought it was the weather, and sleeping outdoors...but then it got even stranger, and I had a horrible dream. These huge men with dark eyes, dark hair…pale faces, really pale."

Everyone looked at one another. *Pale faces?* That usually indicated vamps.

"I got angry. Furious. Like I wanted to destroy things. Everyone was running wild, smashing stuff up — it was mayhem. But I don't remember Hazel being like…us. I think she and her friends—she had a brother with her—they ran. I never saw her again. I hope she's okay…"

He trailed off.

"Do you remember more about what these creatures looked like?" I prompted. "Or where they came from?"

The boy shook his head and looked blankly around the room again.

"I don't remember a boat or anything. It was like they appeared out of thin air."

We had found the footsteps by the jetty. If they hadn't come by boat, then maybe there was a portal nearby?

"They could have come from further along the coast," Corrine said. "The ground was muddy—if the humans had run over their tracks, it would be difficult to find the trail."

She was right. The ground had been stampeded by the mindless humans; if there had been clues there, they were now destroyed.

"We need more to go on," Corrine sighed as she escorted

us out of the room. The boy had started to stare blankly at the wall again, and it looked like he was starting to revert to his mindless state.

"What's the likelihood of him having his mind restored?" I asked Corrine as soon as we were out of earshot.

"I think eventually we'll manage to fix him—he needs rest and quiet. It looks like their minds were drained almost entirely of energy. It weakened the frontal lobes and the connectivity between the left and right sides of the brain. In that weakened state, their minds were far more susceptible to 'pack mentality', which might be why they attacked us... I want to make a brief visit to The Sanctuary and tap into their larger pool of knowledge, see if anyone there has any ideas."

"Okay," I said, swallowing. "Well then, we'll continue looking at police reports—we should spread the search as wide as we can."

"We'll help," Claudia replied, and the rest of the parents agreed. We divided up the search locations, and then Caleb and I started to make our way home from the hospital. When we reached our treehouse apartment, my mom was waiting on the balcony.

"Any news?" she asked.

I filled her in on the little information we had, and she nodded.

"I doubt our kids were an isolated incident," she murmured. "If these creatures were feeding off mind energy, then they were successful. They'll probably try again, if they haven't done so already."

"Have Derek and Ben returned yet?" Caleb asked. I'd filled him in on their visit from Sherus, and he'd been just as surprised as I was at the request from the fae.

"Not yet." My mom shook her head with a worried frown. "Though I expected them back by now."

I recalled the description my brother had given me of the fae realm—consisting of four elemental stars that were situated in the In-Between, the strange, dark, vacuum that we had all passed through via portal countless times when travelling between the human and supernatural dimensions. None of us ever ventured into the In-Between—GASP hadn't had reason to—and consequently it remained shrouded in mystery. Other than the fae, we had no idea what creatures lived there, if any.

From the strange figures appearing at Murkbeech to the motivations of Sherus, it felt like we knew too little about everything right now.

HAZEL

I stood staring into the darkness of the passageway.

My brother had just been sucked back into whatever was at the end of its cavernous depths, while I had struggled in Tejus's grip, totally helpless to do anything other than scream. The image of Benedict scrambling around to get a grip on the stones of the wall to stop himself from being dragged backward, his eyes wide with fear, would stay with me forever.

Tejus had loosened his grip on me, but his arms still created a barrier, stopping me from running headlong into the passage after my brother.

"We need to follow him!" I cried out, twisting my body

around to face Tejus. I looked up into his eyes, pleading.

"We don't know what's down there, Hazel," he replied firmly.

"Yes, we do! *Benedict* is down there, and we need to go after him! It's my brother. I know that doesn't mean much to you, but it means something to me."

I regretted the words as soon as I said them. Tejus frowned, his mouth tightening. I had hurt him, that was obvious, and it only served to show how reckless I was feeling.

"I'm sorry," I said, "but we don't know if the barrier around the castle is going to stay down. Let's follow him now, before it's too late."

Tejus's jaw twitched, but I could see he was about to relent.

"I'm coming with you," he snapped.

"Okay."

"What?" exclaimed one of the ministers. I thought it sounded like Lithan. "It's sheer madness—"

"Silence," Tejus retorted, holding up a hand to stop the ministers from all chattering in support of Lithan. "Our lack of knowledge on this entity is starting to infuriate me. This human boy may well be the only one among us who knows more than next to nothing about what it wants or what its plans are."

Tejus released me fully from his arms and leaned down to get a better look inside the passage. The torches that I had laid down along either side of the wall had blown out, and Tejus ordered one of the guards to fetch us more. The guard returned a few moments later, carrying two large torches. Tejus handed one to me.

"Stay behind me," he ordered, and took the first step into the narrow passage. He practically had to bend double to walk through it, and I wondered who had built this castle originally—was it sentries as I had originally assumed? There were so many parts of it that seemed more fitting for humans, with narrow arches and small doorways running throughout the servant quarters. I tucked the question away to ask Tejus at a later date—right now I wanted us both focused on bringing Benedict back where he belonged.

The torches threw shadows along the passage, and soon the light from the hallway behind us dimmed completely and only darkness lay ahead. Other than the sound of our footsteps, and the short exhales of irritation from Tejus as his back scraped along the damp stone, there was silence.

"How long do you think this thing goes on for?" I asked, more to break the oppressive silence than anything else.

"I'm not sure," Tejus replied. "The passage isn't included

on any of the castle blueprints I found. Either it originates from before the castle came into existence, or it was kept secret for a reason. Possibly both."

"Is there anything the ministers here *don't* keep secret?"

Tejus grunted in agreement. "They have been given far too much power by my father and the rulers before him. I intend to put a stop to that. Eventually."

When I become emperor, was the unspoken implication. I hoped that he would put a stop to the ministers' secrets. They had caused enough damage already.

We walked a little further in silence, and soon I could see light coming from up ahead.

"What's that?" I breathed. It wasn't the yellowish glow of torchlight that I might have expected. Instead, the lights were piercingly bright, and reflected off the walls of the passage in a myriad of different colors: reds, golds, pinks and greens, all dancing in the darkness.

Tejus didn't answer me, but we simultaneously picked up the pace. The lights grew brighter, almost blinding, until Tejus came to an abrupt halt in front of me. I peered around him with difficulty—the passage was so narrow I could barely see past his broad frame. In front of us was a stone wall, a single piece of granite that held an elaborate pattern of stones. They flickered at intervals, creating a hypnotic swirling form of bright colors. I stared at it, dumbstruck.

The stones.

"We've found the lock, haven't we?" I asked Tejus quietly.

"I think so."

He reached out, locating two grooves where stones were clearly missing from the formation.

"Two missing," he said softly.

"How many stones do you think need to be removed until it's unlocked, all of them?"

"I'm not sure. I suppose there's no way of knowing, perhaps until it's too late." He removed his fingers from the grooves and started to run his hands along the top and sides of the granite wall. There was no alternate pathway that Benedict could have taken—somehow he must have passed through the wall.

"Can we open it?" I asked.

"I don't think so." Tejus heaved against it, but the wall didn't even shudder at the force. It appeared to be held tight.

"I think I heard it move," I continued, "when Benedict disappeared. There was a slam—the sound of stone moving...there *must* be a way to get it open."

"I heard it too," Tejus replied, "but I imagine it's under control of the entity. I'll send the ministers in to see if they can be of more help... but I'm afraid we're blocked off."

"There must be a way," I insisted, squeezing past his body to get closer to the stones. I fumbled around the edges of the wall, seeing if there were any small cracks or an indication of how it might have opened that Tejus had missed. I found nothing.

"We can't be blocked off," I said. "Benedict got through here—it will open somehow."

"Benedict is under the control of the entity, Hazel. Clearly it wants him to travel freely through the passageway, but we are definitely blocked off."

I thumped the wall in frustration. The stones continued to glimmer and sparkle. I irrationally felt like they were teasing me, like stupid little pixies laughing at our efforts to get past.

"We need to head back." Tejus' breath was cool on the back of my neck, and I was suddenly aware of our physical closeness. Under any other circumstances it would have felt claustrophobic, but with Tejus in such close proximity I felt my stomach churn and flutter.

Really inappropriate, Hazel, I scolded myself.

Suddenly I was more inclined to move back out of the passageway.

"You go first," I muttered, too shy to squeeze past him again. Tejus started to walk back the way we'd come, and I dutifully followed, looking back at the stones every now and then, still a little entranced by their beauty.

"The stone from the Hellswan sword," I said. "I think it was one of those—the size was about right. It just didn't glow as brightly."

"I agree. It confirms the theory that my father removed one of them to assist Jenus in the trials," Tejus replied, and then muttered an expletive under his breath that I doubted was for my hearing.

The way back felt shorter, and it seemed that we were stepping out into the hallway in nearly half the time. Most of the humans had gone back to their quarters, but Yelena stood opposite the passage with her back against the wall, avoiding making eye contact with the ministers.

"What happened?" she asked, wide-eyed.

"He's gone. We can't follow—there's a wall blocking the way that Benedict must have been able to pass through," I replied. Turning back to Tejus, I prepared myself for another argument.

"We need to go out and look for him outside the castle," I insisted.

Tejus crossed his arms and glared down at me.

"Absolutely not. It's the middle of the night. We're better off looking for him in the morning."

"But that's my point!" I said. "It's the middle of the night—he's going to be somewhere on his own, in the dark…he's going to be so afraid."

Tejus sighed. "He's done this before—he's been doing this for a while now." He glanced over at Yelena, who nodded miserably. "He'll be fine for one evening. We'll go out at daybreak tomorrow, I promise."

In his eyes I read a warning. There would be no persuading him this time. I looked around at the ministers, staring at us as I pleaded with their king.

"The morning, then," I relented.

I received a nod from Tejus, and an intense look that I couldn't quite understand—gratitude, perhaps?

"Lithan, Qentos," Tejus barked at his ministers, "inspect the wall—see if there's any way we can open it. I am escorting Hazel to my quarters, and will rejoin you shortly."

The ministers started shuffling toward the passageway, and I took Yelena's hand.

"We should take her back first," I murmured to Tejus. She looked exhausted and red-eyed, the events of tonight having been way too much for her to handle—more than any of us could handle…except perhaps Tejus, who looked as determined and inscrutable as he always did.

We walked past the emperor's room, and then on the

opposite wall, the writing that Benedict had created with his own blood.

"To follow me is death. But I shall come. I shall come back to claim you."

It had been a message directed at Yelena, but I supposed it had meaning for us all. Tejus had said that we didn't understand the plans of the entity, but to me, this made it clear. My fear for Benedict was overwhelming, weighing on me till I thought it would crush the breath from my body, but it was accompanied with a fear for us all. I didn't like the ministers, and I didn't respect them, but they—and the guards, the rest of the sentries in Nevertide and all the human children under the castle's protection—were in grave danger.

I worried about Tejus too.

He might have seemed unbreakable to me most of the time—the man, or creature, who would protect me with his own life in a heartbeat. But the more we saw of the entity's power, the more fallible and human Tejus became in my eyes. And the more I loved him for it.

"Will you take me with you tomorrow?" Yelena asked as we reached her door.

"No," I replied firmly. "It's too dangerous. I need you to stay here and look after the rest of the kids with Jenney, okay?"

"Okay," she whispered.

She turned to open the door, but then paused.

"Will he be back for me *tonight?*" she asked, her voice hitching in fear as she began to tremble in front of the door.

"No!" I exclaimed, pulling her back round to face me. I pushed her hair back from her face and gazed solemnly down at her. "You're going to be safe here. Tejus will put guards and ministers outside the door. Benedict's after the stones, not you."

What am I saying?

In what crazy world was my brother a figure of fear for a young girl? I felt sick.

"I know it's not him," she replied softly.

I nodded, unable to speak for a moment. Yelena flung her arms around me fiercely.

"We'll find him tomorrow," I reassured her. "We'll bring him back."

"I know," she whispered against my hair, before untangling herself from the embrace and slipping back into her quarters.

"We will find him, right?" I asked Tejus, watching the closing door.

"We'll try."

"Just lie to me, okay?" I retorted through gritted teeth.

"We'll find him and he'll be fine," Tejus lied softly.

BEN

The morning after his unexpected visit, Sherus had requested that my father and I join him for a meeting that was taking place in the fae kingdom. We were standing at the peak of Mount Logan, Canada. Mona had transported us here from The Shade and stood a few paces back from the two of us, staring down into the starry, swirling blackness of the portal. My father looked out over the mountain range and the cloud mists that hung miles below us. We were both wearing black GASP uniforms, and our figures stood out starkly against the white snow. The mountain brought back memories that I would rather forget—the tasks that I'd had to accomplish to earn my ticket out of The Underworld. The uncertainty that

River and I had faced when we'd believed I might never return to her in physical form. It was fair to say that my feelings toward Sherus were complicated.

"I wonder how long we'll need to—"

Before my father could finish his sentence, Sherus stepped out of the portal and onto the snow. He was accompanied by two other fae, who I suspected were guards—heavily armed, with their expressionless gazes fixed on the three of us.

"Thank you for coming." Sherus bowed his head politely.

My father nodded, a touch stiff, but not unmannered.

Sherus's eyes flicked to Mona.

"Our guards will escort Benjamin and Derek the rest of the way. Your services are no longer required."

Mona nodded stiffly. "Call me when you need to return," she muttered to my father and me. After casting one last suspicious look at the fae, she vanished.

With Mona gone, we were alone with these fae, and the idea made me feel slightly uncomfortable.

My father stepped closer to the portal.

"I will lead," Sherus asserted, and gently lowered himself down into the crater. Feeling the suction, my father grabbed hold of my shoulders to stop himself from hurtling downward—since I could fly as a fae, I could resist the pull.

We followed Sherus gradually, with the guards floating down behind us. I looked at the translucent, bluish smoky walls of the portal that surrounded us, and resisted the urge to touch them until it was required. It had been a long time since I'd passed through them.

We followed Sherus down a few feet further, and then he stopped.

"Here," he commanded, and pushed himself right through the swirling walls.

I did the same, still supporting my father, and soon we were hovering in the silent vacuum of the In-Between.

"Behold the empire of the fae," Sherus said softly, pointing up at four globes that created a gentle arc in the black sky. Each glowed softly: white for the air kingdom, blue for the water kingdom, golden-brown for the earth kingdom, and a red hue that marked where we would be headed—the kingdom of fire.

"It has been a long time since we have entertained guests," he continued, eyeing us. "But it is now a must."

We drifted from the tunnel, moving closer to the fae kingdom. I recalled the time I had come here as a spirit, how frightening it had seemed, leaving the tunnel and drifting out into the great abyss. Even now, with my father with me and the fae as our escorts, I didn't want to look back and see the reassuring form of the tunnel disappearing from view.

Our journey took a while, though it might have seemed longer because of the lack of landmarks and the oppressive, unrelenting silence of this strange in-between world. I heaved a sigh of relief when we eventually entered the atmosphere of the fire kingdom. We were all cast in a warm, red glow that blinded us for a few moments as we passed through, and looking down I could see a bustling city, with a large palace rising up to meet us.

We landed lightly in the palace gardens.

"That was something," my father muttered, and I nodded in agreement.

Sherus didn't stop, but moved forward in the direction of the palace, expecting us to follow. I glanced around at a vast lawn with multiple pathways, winding their way through red-leaved trees and small, decorative rockeries of ruby, carnelian and dark ochre topaz. As we moved closer to the impressively large doors, the pathway widened and six fountains marked the final trajectory—three on either side of us. Their heat was immense, and I realized that instead of water emerging from the fountains, huge bursts of brilliant white flame leapt up into the air. I must have stopped and gaped, because Sherus glanced back at me and then turned toward the fountains.

"It was a trick my father learned from the jinn. They can actually create ice fires—this is merely a replica, a trick of the eye."

I nodded, impressed. I'd never seen a jinni create an ice fire, and I wondered how Sherus's father had ever found that out. The jinn and fae weren't exactly close—even after Cyrus Drizan's death so many years ago, the jinn of The Dunes were nobody's allies.

Sherus continued leading us forward. The vast doors opened, their gleaming steel exterior reflecting the fires back to us so it looked as if we were entering some huge white inferno. Inside, the palace was just as impressive. The structure was created from the same polished steel as the doors, but every piece of furnishing, ornament and tile seemed to be created from the same semi-precious stones I'd seen in the garden. It was beautiful indeed, but overwhelming—and I couldn't imagine living in a place where everything was constantly tainted with a soft, red-golden glow. It brought a whole new meaning to 'rose-tinted glasses.'

We were escorted through the palace, and, after ascending a grand staircase, we stopped in front of another large set of doors.

"This is the council chamber," Sherus announced. "I have

called the rulers of the three other kingdoms to meet here today, to discuss my…premonition." He frowned, clearly deliberating about what he was about to say next. "The other rulers don't take too kindly to outsiders." He looked at me and grimaced. "Even if one is in the form of a fae. Be warned—things may get a little unpleasant."

My father and I exchanged a glance, our brows raised. We knew well enough already that the fae tended to keep to themselves, but Sherus's warning didn't exactly make us feel welcome.

Sherus nodded to the guards, and they opened the doors. Sherus led the way through, and we entered a large, airy chamber. In the middle of the floor was a huge pit of fire, and around it stood three other fae kings, each dressed in robes that matched the colors of their element kingdoms.

Sherus went to stand at the head of the fire pit, with my father and I following.

"Brothers." Sherus bowed to the waiting men. "May I present Derek and Benjamin Novak of The Shade."

The rulers nodded politely in our direction, but their expressions were stern and just as unwelcoming as Sherus had warned they might be.

"What is the meaning of this meeting, Sherus?" one of them asked in a clipped tone. "You spoke of danger, but I

see none—and I hear of less. My council suspects a fools'
meeting, but I am giving you the benefit of the doubt."

I expected Sherus to reply in anger, but his expression
remained calm and he addressed the king in a measured tone.

"Patience, Sahaero. I bring you here to tell you what is
writ in the stars. Lately I see bad omens everywhere I look,
and I can't shake the feeling that something is coming—
something that will tear kingdoms apart."

The kings were silent for a few moments, some looking
down into the pit of fire, and some gazing at Sherus with
barely concealed irritation.

"You are not the only star-gazer here, Sherus," another
king remarked. "My people have seen nothing, and neither
have I."

Sherus slowly shook his head.

"I have seen it—there is something erupting in another
dimension. Something that needs to be stopped before it is
too late."

The fae might not have believed Sherus, but his words
sent icy shivers down my spine. I didn't know if there was
any truth behind his words, but I did know that *he* believed
it, and that kind of conviction was hard to ignore.

"The delusions of paranoia," Sahaero muttered. His robes
were white, and I assumed he was the ruler of the air

kingdom.

"Sahaero," another king interrupted. "Peace! I want to hear what Sherus has to say—and why he has brought outsiders to our meeting." The king glared at us both, but his outburst silenced Sahaero.

"Ierde," Sherus addressed the green-robed king, "I want the Novaks to assist us in trying to understand what exactly this threat is. My knowledge is limited—I only know what I feel and what I see in the stars. The Novaks and their army have a great reputation on Earth and in the supernatural dimension for achieving the impossible, bringing peace where others wish bloodshed."

"We have never aligned ourselves with outsiders," Ierde replied, and Sahaero nodded in agreement.

"For good reason," Sherus agreed. "Until now. I believe our isolation policy will do us no favors here. We are about to confront a great threat, and I do not know for sure that we alone have the power to stop it."

More silence ensued, and I risked a glance at my father, who looked faintly skeptical.

Eventually the last king spoke up.

"We have heard you, Sherus," he said. "We need time to think on what has been said. You ask a great deal of us—a great deal of trust. Let us reconvene at another date, and we will determine how we should proceed."

The kings bowed their heads, and Sherus sighed.

"Let it not be too long," he replied quietly.

While the kings remained with their heads bowed, Sherus nodded toward the door. It opened and a guard appeared, waiting for us. My father and I left the silent kings, and stepped out into the hallway. A few moments later we were joined by Sherus, and to my surprise, he was smiling.

"All things considered, that did not go badly," he informed us as we descended the staircase.

What?

Sherus smirked at my expression.

"The fae are different, Benjamin. We tend to take our time on decisions—rarely acting rashly."

Like making an impossible deal with ghouls? Oh, please.

"Think what you like of us," he continued, "and of my warnings. But I tell you that there is danger coming, and your Earth will not be immune. With or without the support of the kings I intend to fight this—but I do wish for your help to discover what it is we will be up against. Will you help me?"

My father, still frowning, looked at me before nodding to the fae.

"We will help you, Sherus," he replied.

Hazel

As promised, at the crack of dawn, Tejus knocked on the door to my bedroom. I was already bathed and dressed, and though I'd only gotten a few hours of sleep the night before, I felt clear-headed and was absolutely convinced that we would find Benedict today and bring him back. I would do whatever it took.

"Good morning," he said as I opened the door.

That's a first.

I drank in the sight of Tejus, with dark shadows under his eyes and a brooding expression on his face. He was dressed in his usual sentry attire, black pants and shirt with his long hair knotted at the back with a leather clasp. Combined with the dark stubble on his jaw where he obviously hadn't shaved for a few days, the effect was startlingly attractive, and it took me a few moments to collect myself and refocus.

"Same to you," I managed, heat rising in my cheeks.

I caught him looking at me with the same level of inspection, starting with my face and roving downward, his eyes becoming darker and more intent as the silence between us grew. Unable to handle his scrutiny for much longer, I cleared my throat.

"We should…" I began.

"Yes," he muttered, and reluctantly turned back toward the living room. He strode over to the table and lifted up a large sheet of parchment.

"These are the most comprehensive blueprints of the castle and the surrounding area," he began to explain as I made my way over. "The passage that Benedict entered isn't marked, but should be here." He placed his finger down on the paper, near where the emperor's quarters were marked. "I am presuming that the passage predates the origins of the castle, and if that's the case then the passage will likely be straight—it would have been easier to create that way, with more rudimentary tools."

Unsheathing his sword, he laid it across the page, aligning it with where the passage began. I traced my finger along the paper, carefully avoiding the blade. Directly ahead of the passage lay miles of forest, and then a small cove.

"What's that?" I asked.

"That's the place I showed you—where we found the temple."

"The temple of the Acolytes?" I asked sharply.

"Yes."

An 'I told you so' seemed redundant, though it was on the tip of my tongue. I had known that the Acolyte cult had something to do with all this, but Tejus hadn't listened to me, always saying that they had disbanded centuries ago.

"We don't know—" Tejus began, but I silenced him with a glare.

"We can *assume*," I replied heatedly.

"Fine," he retorted.

I rolled my eyes and turned back to the map. I did wonder why Tejus had been so reluctant to consider the obvious possibility that the Acolytes were behind this—or at least playing a part.

"Tejus—" I began, but was interrupted by a knock on the door. He moved swiftly to open it, and a guard entered the threshold.

"Your highness, the announcement of the start date of the imperial trials is due to take place at The Fells this morning.

As the barriers around Hellswan seem to be permanently removed, the Impartial Ministers decree that any absence will be an instant disqualification."

Tejus nodded curtly.

"Tell Lithan and Qentos that their presence will be required. I will meet them there shortly."

He shut the door and hastily made his way to his bedroom, returning a moment later, throwing on his robes.

"What about the search?" I demanded.

He glanced up at me as he strode back toward the door. "This won't take long. We will resume the search as soon as I am done. I promised you, Hazel—I'm not going to break my word."

"Can I come with you?" I asked quickly. "Then we can go straight from this Fells place, and we won't waste time."

Tejus paused, considering my request.

"You will not speak to anyone when we arrive, and you will not offer your opinion on any matter discussed, is that clear?" His voice was laced with warning.

"It's clear," I snapped back.

We glared at each other for a moment, before the corner of Tejus's mouth twitched ever so slightly.

"Let's go." He turned away from me, and if I hadn't known better I would have thought that he was laughing.

I followed Tejus dutifully across the castle till we reached the courtyard. He stood still for a few moments before his vulture landed gracefully a few feet in front of us. I braced myself for another terrifying ride, and hoped that it would at least be a short one.

"What are The Fells anyway?" I asked as Tejus lifted me up onto the back of the humongous bird. He jumped up behind me, and in one smooth motion the bird spread its wings and lifted up into the air as Tejus wrapped his arms tightly around my waist. I leaned back against his chest, feeling safe surrounded by his arms and the steady beat of his heart as the bird soared higher into the sky.

"The Fells are over there." He released one arm from my waist and pointed up ahead. "They're the geographical center point where all the kingdoms meet, so it's often used for conferences between the rulers."

I nodded, not really caring about the answer to my question as my mind whirred with thoughts of Tejus—embarrassingly conjuring up images of the time I had seen him naked in the labyrinth, and, more recently, wearing only a towel around his waist. He had told me before that he could sense when I was near him, our connection growing stronger with every mind-meld, but I hoped that he wasn't engaging in complete mind-reading without my even knowing.

"Are all the kingdoms taking part in the imperial trials?" I asked, trying to distract myself.

"As far as I know, yes. They are."

"Any stiff competition?" I teased.

I felt Tejus's chest rumble with repressed laughter.

"No," he replied.

I found myself smiling as the bird started to descend toward a break in the trees, and I instantly felt guilty. I shouldn't be enjoying spending time with Tejus when Benedict was all alone somewhere, possessed by some malevolent creature. I vowed that for the rest of the day I would remove unwanted thoughts about Tejus as soon as they popped up.

A moment later I got a chance to test my newfound willpower as he jumped down from the bird, and reached back up to lift me off. His hands circled my waist, then rose higher as gravity pulled me down. When my feet were planted firmly on the ground, his hands stayed where they were a beat longer than was necessary, and I stepped backward, almost toppling over the large claw of the vulture.

I righted myself, and, avoiding looking at Tejus, I turned my attention to the scene before me. We had landed in a small meadow, with the wild thickets of forest surrounding the grassland causing it to be cast in shade. Directly in the middle there was a crumbling and ivy-strewn pavilion made of white stone. It had a domed top and wide arches that made up its circumference. Ministers were standing around in their dark cloaks, wrapped tightly to shield them from the damp weather. I saw Queen Trina standing under one of the arches, and my skin prickled in anger. She was talking to a wizened old man with a long beard that reached down to the floor. As I scanned the rest of the sentries gathered, I noticed five others just like him, all hunched over with age, all wearing thick, snow-white facial hair.

"Who are they?" I asked Tejus quietly, recalling his strict instructions not to talk before we'd left the castle.

"They're the Impartial Ministers," he replied, and I remembered the guard mentioning them. "They will judge the imperial trials—they live like monks in an old ruin not far from here, and are the ultimate ministerial authority." He smirked. "Some say they are immortal. I don't believe that, but they have been around for a long time."

"Do they advise you, like the other ministers?" I asked, catching sight of Lithan and Qentos approaching the pavilion.

"No. They only advise other ministers. They are *supposed* to be completely impartial, guiding only by what is right for

Nevertide as a whole, hence their name."

"But can't we speak to them about what's been going on at Hellswan? They might know more than the others," I declared. Judging by the look of them, they had probably been around before the castle was built.

"My ministers would have already consulted them," Tejus replied grimly. "As king, I am not permitted to seek out their advice."

I pursed my lips in frustration. Like the rest of Tejus's ministers, I didn't really trust Lithan or Qentos. It wasn't so much anything they'd done exactly—it was more their general muttering and apparent lack of knowledge that made me question their ability and willingness to help their king.

Queen Trina moved to speak with another of the ministers, and as she did so, I caught a glimpse of Ash at the back of the pavilion.

"Ash is there!" I turned to Tejus. "I need to speak to him—I'll be back." I rushed off without waiting for an answer, which I imagined would be a 'no' I was going to ignore anyway. I avoided the sentries, giving the pavilion a wide berth as I made my way to Ash.

He was standing alone looking pensive, but when he saw me, his expression broke into a broad grin.

"Hey, you," he greeted. I smiled—Ash's Americanisms

were coming along.

"Hey, how's Ruby?" I asked. "Is she okay?"

He nodded. "She's fine. Safe. We've been staying in the Seraq kingdom since the night the barrier came up around Hellswan. I thought Tejus had erected it at first, which is why we left...but Ruby thought otherwise. It was the entity, right?"

I nodded, glad that Ruby had stuck up for Tejus.

"So are you working with Queen Trina now?"

"I'm helping her with the imperial trials – strategy mostly, and syphoning when it's permitted."

I tried to smile, glad that Ash was no longer working in the kitchen, but I wasn't entirely convinced of my friend's safety if she was staying with Queen Trina.

"I thought that might be the case—Jenney mentioned that you might. I saw you leave that night – I tried to call out...but, well – it was pointless. I don't want Ruby to think I abandoned her...But now that the barriers are opened, are you both going to stay with...the queen?" I asked as politely as I could.

Ash gave a short bark of laughter. "Another fan of hers, I take it?"

I glanced toward the pavilion. "Let's not go there. I know you want Ruby with you, but please tell her that Tejus will come and get her if she ever wants to come back."

"He will, will he?" Ash remarked, looking skeptical.

"He will," I asserted.

"All right. I'll tell her." He smiled crookedly. I wasn't sure if it was my imagination or not, but the light seemed to dim from his eyes.

"How are you?" he asked after a pause.

I swallowed.

I'm not good.

"Benedict's missing…well, not exactly *missing* – he left the castle. I think he's in an old temple by the cove…Tejus and I are going there after this."

Ash looked horrified, and it was a reminder to me just how bad things had gotten since Hellswan Castle had been blocked off by the borders. I had left out the part about the entity taking him…I wasn't sure I wanted it reaching anyone else's ears, especially not Queen Trina's and it would only worry Ruby half to death.

"When you find Benedict, get out of that castle, Hazel. Both of you."

I shook my head. "I can't," I whispered. Ash glanced in the direction of Tejus and nodded with bleak understanding.

"I should get back. Tell her I love her," I said softly.

"'Course," he muttered.

"Thanks Ash."

He nodded and then fixed his gaze back on the pavilion. I felt awkward suddenly, like I was speaking to the enemy or something, and hurried back to join Tejus. I was aware that I'd started to resent Ash a little bit...I understood that working for Queen Trina was probably a really good career move for him, but I couldn't help the irrational feeling that he'd somehow betrayed Tejus, and taken my best friend away from me when I needed her the most. It was selfish of me to think like that, but the feelings were there all the same. Ash was right about one thing though – if I wasn't willing to leave Hellswan to stay elsewhere in Nevertide, as soon as Benedict was free then I would give *him* that option. Not with Queen Trina, but perhaps there was somewhere else that wasn't constantly under threat. Just until we could get out of here for good.

"Please, kings and queen of Nevertide, assemble." A quiet but firm voice echoed from the pavilion, and the sentries started to move—the ministers shuffling back while some stepped up onto the stone, taking their place beneath the arches. I watched as Tejus took the arch nearest where I was standing, with Lithan and Qentos standing directly behind him. I tried to get a better vantage point, but they were all so tall it was near impossible without getting too close.

In a matter of moments, the six royals were each standing beneath individual arches, while the six Impartial Ministers stood in the center of the dome. I couldn't really make out the faces of any of the royals, but from a distance they all seemed as tall and broad as Tejus, with Queen Trina looking as fragile as a china doll in comparison. *Eugh.*

"Welcome all." The old minister spoke again. "We meet in grave times indeed. Perilous times. Which is why the imperial trials have more importance than ever before; our land is in need of a leader, someone to bring us into a new dawn. A new age."

He paused. Everyone waited in complete silence—even the whispering of the ministers had ceased completely.

"Thus, the trials will begin tomorrow at daybreak. We will reconvene here, and you will receive further instruction."

This time a wave of muttering went up through the waiting ministers that surrounded the pavilion. I moved closer, trying to see what kind of reaction the kings were having to the news. I could only get within a yard of the structure without pushing through the sentries and drawing attention to myself. From my vantage point, Queen Trina's face was the only one visible to me, and she looked gleeful.

"Please note," the minister continued, "due to the circumstances, there will be no witnesses to the trials. No audiences, no crowds, no others than yourselves and two chosen ministers; their names should be delivered to one of us before the sun sets."

The sentries started moving again, and the murmurs grew louder. Obviously the meeting was over, and as the ministers parted, Tejus stepped down from the pavilion. As I made my way over to him, I couldn't help but pick up on snippets of conversation the sentries were having amongst themselves.

"Red rains… Hellswan bastard, they've been too long in power…the runes have been writ…time is short…can't remove the borders…just plain trickery! Treachery!"

It frightened me how unpopular Tejus was. If this was what the ministers thought, then surely the Impartial Ministers would feel the same way? What if they swayed the trials in favor of the other kings—or worse, Queen Trina?

I approached Tejus. He was speaking to another man who, judging by his elaborate sword and colored cloak, was a king of one of the other kingdoms.

"It is insanity!" the king hissed. "We need to delay the trials—I fear for our kingdoms, and this is just a distraction! What can they possibly be thinking?"

"They're thinking that the kingdoms need to be united, Thraxus. I agree with them—these are dangerous times, and we need to stand united."

The king threw his hands up in the air, "Of course you say that, Hellswan! The danger comes from *your* kingdom. I have heard mad stories! Old stories, tales long forgotten but by the old ones…" The king shook his head warily, backing away from Tejus.

I looked up at Tejus. He didn't look offended in the slightest, just resigned as he watched the retreating king.

"Hey," I whispered.

He smirked down at me. "You can talk now."

I rolled my eyes. "I was being polite. I didn't want to intrude."

"A first," he quipped, smiling at his own joke.

I chose to ignore him, and began to walk away from the surrounding ministers, hoping that he would follow me. He did.

"Why are you pleased the trials are starting?" I asked as soon as we were out of earshot. "Aren't you worried? There are more apocalyptic signs to come, there's an entity trying to escape from your castle…I mean, I can think of a million reasons why it would be a good idea to postpone them."

Tejus shook his head.

"We need that book. We *need* an emperor. Otherwise, that entity is going to rise from whatever prison it was put in, and there's going to be nothing to halt its ascension. Nevertide will be lost." He paused, gently brushing a stray hair from my forehead, and smiled sadly at me. "And all who reside within it."

TEJUS

I stepped back, my hand burning from where I'd brushed against her temple. As ever with Hazel, her mind called to me in a way I found almost impossible to comprehend. I had syphoned off many minds in my lifetime—so many, each with their unique fabric and texture. None had affected me the way Hazel's had, and never before had I been tempted into something as intimate as our 'mind-meld'—the term she used to describe our practice of sharing memories and visions.

When we had arrived at the Fells, the group of waiting ministers from the Nevertide kingdoms and Hazel's questions about the Impartial Ministers had given me an idea. It related to something I had originally dismissed out of hand, but the more time I spent with Hazel, the more it tugged at my mind—and could no longer be ignored.

"I need to attend to something. Will you wait here for me?" I asked Hazel courteously. I knew how eager she was to get to her brother, but I didn't know when I'd get another chance to do what needed to be done.

"Uh…yeah," she breathed. Color had risen in her cheeks, distracting me once again. How much time could I spend around Hazel without being permitted to touch her the way I wanted to? It was testing my sanity every passing moment, and it was becoming increasingly impossible to find the will to restrain myself.

"I won't be long," I replied, and then left her standing by my vulture. I searched the departing crowds, looking for a preferable candidate. So many of the ministers I found intolerable, and my own weren't exempt from that judgment. Averting my eyes from Queen Trina, who was knowingly smiling at me in a way I found repugnant, I saw King Memenion talking to one of his ministers—a sentry of fairly high regard, who had been in the service of Memenion for decades. I waited until their conversation came to a close, and Memenion walked away from the pavilion.

I approached the minister swiftly, ignoring the bemused

stares of Ashbik and another of Queen Trina's sidekicks.

"Tarkus," I called, before he could turn back to join his king.

He turned to me in faint surprise before resuming a placid expression.

"King Tejus." He bowed. "To what do I owe the honor?"

I glanced around us before replying. The pavilion was empty, but I drew him toward one of the arches, using the stonework to offer us some privacy.

"A question," I replied.

"I am not at liberty to discuss the trials with you, your highness."

"It doesn't concern the trials," I reassured him. "I wanted some information. I have heard rumors of a transformative effect occurring when another species marries a sentry royal. Are they true?"

Tarkus's face turned a puce color and he looked over my shoulder in the direction of Hazel.

"You can't be serious!" he exploded.

"The question is hypothetical," I replied through gritted teeth. I wanted to reprimand him for his insolence, but I needed answers more than gratification.

"I would hope so, your highness. Your reputation would be at stake; forgive my unruly tongue, but you are already under suspicion by many, and the Hellswan name, as I'm sure you know, is not as…immaculate as it might be."

"Hold that tongue before you lose it," I replied curtly. "I know all this. I came to you for information—will you give it to me or not?"

Tarkus bowed his head again, his color slowly returning to normal.

"Forgive me… These times are tense, lesser men let the madness get to them." He sighed. "You are referring to other species becoming sentries, correct?"

I nodded.

"As far as I am aware, it is a specific part of the marriage ceremony that is the catalyst for the transformation."

I listened to his words, my heart sinking. I had half hoped that it was all some strange myth—tales told of old magic that no longer existed. I would have preferred Tarkus to have laughed at me and called me a fool than reply with solemnity.

"What part of the ceremony, specifically?" I asked dully.

Tarkus eyed me warily.

"I am not sure, exactly. But there is a part of the ceremony, as I am sure you know, where the appointed minister binds heart, soul, spirit and mind. During this ritual, both sentries will typically syphon off one another. When that part of the ceremony is conducted by a sentry and a non-sentry, the abilities of the sentry are somehow transferred to the other species. I believe this is the moment that the transformation takes place."

One part of the ceremony. One ritual.

Would a marriage still be binding if that ritual was missed or altered in some way?

"Has it happened in recent history?" I asked.

"Not for many centuries. The last known record was a nymph who married a king. She took on sentry-like qualities."

"Which king?" I asked with interest.

"A long-dead king of the Thraxus kingdom. It is the only record I know of, though perhaps there are more in the archives. I can inquire with the Impartial Ministers if it would please you, your Highness?"

"No," I replied swiftly. I had trusted Tarkus because I'd heard that he remained silent on private matters, and Memenion held him in high regard. The Impartial Ministers I did *not* trust. "That will be all. Thank you for the information."

Tarkus correctly recognized my words as a dismissal, and left me standing alone in the pavilion.

My torture felt complete.

A small voice in the back of my mind considered the

possibility of not marrying Hazel at all. Perhaps, if it were enough, she would be willing to stay with me anyway…I dismissed the idea immediately. I was a king. I hoped to be an emperor. It would be impossible. My people and the other kingdoms already doubted me—already questioned my relationship with Hazel. To keep her on as some sort of mistress would be abhorrent.

Another option would be to tell her. To give her the choice—let her know that if she wanted to be with me, it would come at a cost. A great cost. I thought of her dislike of Nevertide—the constant fear and uncertainty she'd faced since she'd arrived, how the sentries she'd met had either put her life in danger or toyed with her for their own purposes, like me. How could I possibly ask her to become one of them? She had a different destiny waiting, didn't she? Her family were supernatural vampires. Surely she would want to join their race—leave her human life behind for immortality.

I turned my head to watch her from the pavilion. She was observing the bird, tentatively reaching out to stroke the soft feathers on its forehead.

Could she adapt to this life?

In my heart, I doubted it—perhaps *knew* that she couldn't.

What I could offer her in return was so little: the grey skies and castle of Hellswan, a kingdom that literally hated my name, and my own unpracticed, possessive version of love. It wasn't enough. Not for what she would have to give up in return.

I thought again of what Tarkus had said. That it was only one part of the ceremony that caused the transformation, in theory. As emperor, would I dare to change the ceremony, to remove the ritual and declare us legally married?

If Hazel was willing—willing and clear as to what little I could offer her—perhaps I could.

I gazed around at the crumbling, ivy-infested stone of the pavilion; the center of Nevertide looked as old and tired as I felt. All my life I had hoped to rule this land. And now the stakes were even higher.

RUBY

I'd sat in our appointed room for most of the day. I'd tried to venture out a few times, but only ended up getting lost and luckily bumping into a sentry who could direct me. The nymph from last night hadn't made a reappearance either. I was quite glad about that; I'd tried to tell Ash last night about my second sighting, but he'd just shrugged it off, leaving me feeling frustrated and utterly alone.

For the first time since I met Ash, I had really started to feel the sentry-and-human divide. It was as if Queen Trina's attentions had lessened his anger toward Nevertide politics and royalty, but that anger toward the status quo had always been one of the things that had made him seem more human to me.

This morning he had left early, claiming that he needed to accompany Queen Trina to a meeting about the imperial trials. He'd left in such a hurry he hadn't even bothered to tell me where it was, or how long he would be gone.

I desperately wanted to get out of this castle. But at the same time I didn't want to leave Ash behind.

Good luck with that.

It was obvious that he was in his element here. As much as I didn't like it—and didn't trust Queen Trina—it kind of felt like Ash was here to stay. I didn't know where that left us.

I heard a fumbling at the door to the room. I was about to ask who it was when Ash peered around the door with a broad smile on his face.

"Hey, shortie. Thought I'd find you in the gardens."

"I kept getting lost." I smiled sheepishly back. "This place is worse than Hellswan."

"Trust me – it's really not," Ash replied.

"You know what I mean," I replied, trying to sound light-hearted. Ash's obvious good mood made me feel even more rejected. Did he no longer care about the plans we'd made to leave Nevertide together? That had been a couple of days ago, and already things seemed different.

"I saw Hazel," Ash said. "She sends her love. But Benedict is missing…again. I'm sure they'll find him, and Julian eventually. I don't blame them for wanting to get out of that place."

"Did he not come home the night of the rain?" I asked, my body tensing.

"I don't know—there wasn't time for details. But she and Tejus were going out to look for him. I'm sure he's fine."

I nodded, but my decision was made.

"Ash, I need to leave. Like, *now.*"

He slumped back against the wall dejectedly, scratching his forehead.

"I knew you'd say that," he muttered.

"I'm sorry. I don't want to leave you here…but I've got to go. Why don't you come with me?" I pleaded.

"I can't, shortie. I need to stay here—help with the trials. She's got a really good chance of winning. Especially if Tejus remains distracted by your friend."

"What?"

He shrugged. "His mind's not on the game. Anyone can see that."

His comment had annoyed me. I tried to remind myself that Ash had always been pretty ruthless—poisoning the emperor to get one up on Jenus, for instance. But this was the first time that it had bothered me.

"My friend's feelings aren't a *game*," I shot back.

His eyes widened at my reply, and he put his arms up in mock-surrender.

"I'm just saying… Anyway, it's Tejus who's the one affected. Hazel just seemed worried about her brother."

"I need to leave. Can you take me back?" I asked, wanting to get our parting over and done with. I knew I was being difficult, but I couldn't seem to help it. Maybe I needed a bit of space to work out exactly what I was feeling…I was pretty sure that my irritation was a mask for something else.

"All right," Ash said. He didn't look at me, just opened the door again and stepped out into the hallway. He started to walk along, not once looking back to see if I was following.

"I have a meeting with Queen Trina, so I can't go with you," he said suddenly. "I'll put you in a carriage though, with a guard. You'll be fine."

"O-Okay…" I tried to hide the hurt in my voice.

We continued walking along the hallways of the palace in silence, till we reached a marble-floored courtyard. Our silence became thicker and increasingly awkward as our footsteps echoed on the stone floor.

Ash let out a low groan.

"Ruby, don't do this!" He spun around to face me, his

face miserable. "Stay and we can look for Benedict in the other kingdoms near here—he could be anywhere! Same with Julian."

I was tempted. I realized that I didn't want to leave Ash. Not just because I was worried about him, but because I didn't want to deal with Nevertide without him. But his interest in Queen Trina and her minister position had hurt my feelings—made me feel unwanted and redundant. I *wanted* to change my mind, but how could I justify leaving Hazel to look for Benedict and Julian by herself? And what about the kids at the castle? They had no one other than us. I had a responsibility toward them.

"I want to, Ash—I really do, but I can't," I replied.

"Will you come back?" he asked.

"Of course. I will—I promise. As soon as all this settles, I'll come back."

"All right then." He sighed. "I just don't want to leave you in Hellswan alone."

"I won't be," I pointed out. "Hazel's there—Jenney too." I didn't even bother mentioning Tejus's name.

"Yeah, but I won't be," he replied softly.

"I'm tougher than I look," I reminded him with a smile.

"That I don't doubt, shortie." He pulled me toward him, and I stepped gratefully into the warmth of his arms. He lowered his head and kissed me softly on the lips, nuzzling his nose against mine as he did so. I raised my arms upward, wanting to draw him closer, and he lifted me with a short laugh. Our lips met again, more forcefully this time, and I sank into his warmth, wanting to stay more than ever.

I was the first to pull back.

"Ash…"

"I know, you need to go," he replied breathlessly. "Let me get a carriage. Wait here."

I stood by the entrance gates to the palace, noticing for the first time how little security Queen Trina had in comparison with Hellswan. Perhaps it was because Hellswan was the seat of the emperor, but it seemed odd that any royal home would be so lax. Shrugging, I turned when I heard the sound of a bull-horse and carriage trotting across the courtyard. A lone guard rode the bull-horse. He must have been in his thirties, with a pale face that looked strangely expressionless and vacant. Ash walked next to the horse, smiling ruefully at me.

"This is Tarq, he'll take you to Hellswan." Ash announced.

The guard nodded in my direction, but I got the distinct impression that he wasn't really seeing me.

"You'll be all right," Ash whispered, "he's harmless."

I nodded, still feeling a little uneasy. Not wanting to make a fuss over nothing, I smiled up at the guard in greeting and climbed into the back of the carriage.

"See you soon," I called out the window.

Ash waved, mouthing something that I couldn't hear over the clattering of the hooves and wheels. I waved back as the guard set off at a brisk pace.

Slumping back in my seat, I watched the manicured lawns and exotic plants of the Seraq kingdom become meadows and then thick forests.

My promise to Abelle, the apothecary who viewed Ash like her son, came back to haunt me—that I would watch his back, and keep a close eye on Queen Trina. But I couldn't ignore the needs of my family. Though Julian, Benedict and Hazel weren't my blood relations, we were a family in the way it counted most. I knew Hazel would be going out of her mind with worry—I needed to be there for her.

The bull-horse started to slow down, and it neighed loudly as it came to an abrupt halt. I peered further out of the window and saw three guards, all heavily armed, approach.

"State your business, Seraqean," one of them commanded. My driver disembarked the carriage.

"I have a passenger for Hellswan," he replied vacantly.

The guards turned in my direction, and I hastily opened the carriage door and stepped out.

"I'm staying at the Hellswan castle," I replied as confidently as I could. "With King Tejus and Hazel Achilles. They're expecting me."

"Stand down," one of the guards barked at the other two. I looked up at him in surprise, and he winked at me.

"You're Ruby. You assisted Ashbik in the trials, correct?" he asked.

"Yes, that's me."

He nodded, a faint smile playing on his lips. He was almost as tall and broad as Tejus, with dark features—and there was something else about him that reminded me of the new king, maybe the sense that he could potentially be as brooding and deadly, but his manner seemed to be easygoing. I couldn't imagine Tejus winking at someone.

"You left the castle?" he asked curiously.

"I went with Ash to visit Queen Trina."

"Ah, of course," he mused, then smiled. "And survived."

Before I could ask what he meant, he leaned past me and reopened the carriage door.

"Hellswan awaits, Ruby."

I clambered inelegantly back into the carriage.

"I'm going to escort Ruby back to the castle myself." He

turned to the other two guards, and they saluted in response.

"As you wish, Commander Varga," one replied.

The name rang a bell—Hazel had mentioned him before, the guard who was in charge of Julian's search party. What was he doing questioning people, at what I presumed were the borders of Hellswan?

The carriage started up again, and a few moments later, Commander Varga came up beside the door, riding his own bull-horse.

"Why aren't you searching for Julian?" I asked, leaning out of the window to catch his attention.

"We were. We've searched high and low." He shook his head in displeasure. "I am very sorry, but we've had to suspend the search for a while. There's been so much happening, we've needed all our man power to calm the villagers, to maintain order."

I realized that I hadn't given much thought to the effects the boundaries and blood rains might have had on the general population.

"People must be terrified," I murmured.

"They are. But it's nothing we can't handle... Not yet, anyway."

The journey carried along in silence for a while, and then Varga smirked down at me.

"You did well in the trials. Both you and Ashbik. You must have an impressive mind."

"Oh, it's Ash who's the impressive one. My mind is totally average."

He looked skeptical. "I doubt that."

"Well, we fell at the last hurdle," I reminded him, thinking back to the final trial where Ash had lost because I'd not been able to provide him with any mental energy.

"I noticed," Varga replied solemnly. "What happened?"

I was silent for a moment. I wasn't really clear on how to answer that question—I was still so unsure myself.

"I don't actually know…" I hesitated.

"Did anyone suspect foul play?" he asked.

"No," I replied, surprised.

Before he could reply, Commander Varga's bull-horse reared up violently, almost throwing him back onto the ground. I could hear the bull-horse driving my carriage neighing and whickering in panic. The buggy swayed to one side, and I was thrown back against the seat. I righted myself and reached for the door, pushing it open.

"Get back in!" Varga roared at me, still trying to calm his bull-horse.

"What's going on?" I asked, pulling the door shut, but leaning as far out of the window as I could.

Varga pulled tightly on the reins of his bull-horse, and it finally settled onto all fours. He moved forward, grabbing the reins off my driver to steady the carriage.

"What in Nevertide is *that?*" Varga muttered.

Ignoring the instructions I'd been given, I stepped out of the carriage and stood in the middle of the road. I glanced in the direction that Varga was facing, and stopped still.

Ahead of us were the forests that surrounded Hellswan. Moving rapidly through the trees came billowing white clouds. I thought it might be a strange low-hanging storm, but as I watched flames appeared to lick at the tops of the trees—but they weren't red or yellow, but a bright bluish white. The white flames had ravaged the forest in their wake, leaving nothing but frosty, dead-limbed trees where flames still danced on their topmost branches. I had never seen anything like it in my life, and I stared dumbstruck as the flames flew closer toward us.

"Change of plan," Varga asserted calmly.

Before I knew what was happening, he leaned down and wrapped his arm around my waist. In one rapid movement he hoisted me up on his bull-horse, setting me down in front of him.

The bull-horse reared up again, and he spun the creature around in the opposite direction. I could see the intense and determined look in his eyes as he bent low over me, kicking the horse with his back legs as we galloped off—getting as much distance as we could between us and the approaching ice inferno.

HAZEL

We headed toward the Viking graveyard, flying as low as we could in the hope of spotting Benedict wandering in the forest. The air was mild at the Fells, but as we approached Hellswan it became still and cold. We circled lower when we approached the cove, and as soon as we caught sight of the muddy sands, a brilliant flash of light momentarily blinded us. A second later, white flames leapt up from the surrounding trees, billowing dry smoke toward us that smacked into my face like shards of glass.

"What on earth is that?" I gasped, leaning forward on the neck of the vulture as I looked down at the forest below.

"I have no idea," Tejus replied in wonder.

He turned the bird away from the oncoming flame, but it seemed to chase us—ice-cold, bluish flickers leaping from one branch to the next, quickly surrounding the cove.

"We need to turn around!" Tejus yelled over the crackling of the leaves and the high-pitched blast of the fire.

"No!" I cried out. I couldn't leave Benedict down there. "We have to land—please, Tejus!"

The flames leapt higher still, and Tejus pulled the bird upward.

"You'll get us killed, Hazel," he growled, holding on to me tightly as the vulture rose.

"I can't leave him!"

"We must!" he shouted, trying to steer the bird away from the cove in the direction of the castle. The bird screamed. It was the most atrocious sound I'd ever heard, more human than animal, and it ripped right through my eardrums.

"Damn!" Tejus yelled, tightening his grip on me as the bird spun out of control. I looked over at its wings, expecting flames to be spreading across its giant feathers. Instead I saw that the tips had frozen, their color turning an icy white, like a frost that was steadily moving up the wing to the creature's body.

"Hazel." Tejus spoke with quiet control in my ear. "You need to hold on. I can't control the bird—it's in too much pain. Whatever you do, *hold on*."

I clutched at the feathers beneath my fingers, my heart racing as the bird flew uncontrollably, spinning and whirring into the sky. I shut my eyes, too scared to see the ground come rushing up to meet us. Its horrific scream continued, and in trying to block it out I became aware only of Tejus's firm chest behind me and the vice-like grip he held me in.

"We're going to land," Tejus called out to me, but I could barely hear him over the rushing wind as the bird picked up speed.

We were too low. Branches swiped at my face as the bird juddered, smacking into the tops of the trees. My stomach jolted as we suddenly dropped lower, free-falling in the air. The bird gave another thunderous squawk, and we hit the ground. I nearly went flying off the creature, but Tejus held on tight around my waist, yanking me back toward him.

A moment later we were still. All I could hear was the sound of my and Tejus's rasping breaths, our thundering hearts and the soft whimpers of the bird beneath us. Slowly I opened my eyes. The surroundings looked familiar, but in my shock I couldn't quite place them.

"Where…where are we?" I stuttered.

"Ghouls' Ridge," Tejus breathed.

I looked around once again and saw the precipice of the

mountain to my right where the trials had taken place, and the steep drop on either side—which I knew was miles deep, ending in swirling mists and jagged rocks.

"That was lucky," I managed, feeling sick at how close we'd come to falling off the edge. We wouldn't have survived the fall.

"It was."

Keeping his arms wrapped around me, Tejus heaved us both off the bird. It gave another whimper as my feet gingerly touched the solid earth beneath us. When he released me, my head spun, and it took me a few moments of deep breathing to right myself.

"Are you hurt?" Tejus asked, taking my shoulders in his hands.

"I'm fine, just a bit dizzy."

"You've been cut. It was probably the branches." Tejus ran his thumb over my bottom lip. He was right. I could taste the coppery tang of blood in my mouth and felt a sharp pain running from my cheekbone down to my lips.

I gazed up into Tejus's concerned eyes, and a jolt of adrenaline shot through my body. The pain of my cut receded completely as I focused on his part-open mouth and dark hollows of his jaw. He ran his thumb up the length of the cut gently, removing the blood. When he had finished, he took his hand away. His thumb was covered in the bright red smear of my blood. He placed it between his own lips and slowly sucked the liquid away.

Oh… my.

I felt like molten liquid was running through my veins. My throat ran dry and I was incapable of doing anything but staring back at Tejus, completely oblivious to anything but his presence and the mind-blowing effect he was having on me.

"You're trembling, are you cold?" he asked, moving his hands to apply pressure on my forearms.

"Um…no," I replied, confused. I hadn't realized I *was* trembling. I looked down at my body, detecting a slight shaking of my hands. I didn't think it had anything to do with the temperature though.

Tejus looked back at the forest, and I could see the dry white smoke of the flames moving closer.

"I need to build a barrier. I don't think there's any other way out."

I looked over to the pathway of the precipice. On the other side of the ridge, the forest was the same—white flames engulfing everything that grew there. We were surrounded.

"Okay." I nodded hastily. "Do you need me?"

"I think so; do you have the energy?" he asked.

I felt like I had bundles of energy; the adrenaline from the flight and Tejus's touch had made my brain running into overdrive.

"Yes, it's fine," I replied. "Take what you need."

He pulled me closer toward him, bringing my head to his chest.

"It's easier this way," he muttered as I stared up at him, puzzled by his sudden willingness for proximity between us—normally we kept a distance from one another when he syphoned off me.

I felt the familiar, feathery-light touches of Tejus's mind meeting mine. This time, we didn't project images or visions to one another. As soon as his mind touched mine, I realized how tired Tejus was: I hadn't been aware of the last few days taking its toll on him—he had obviously hidden it well. I opened my mind up as much as I could, focusing on sending all the energy I could muster up toward him.

He exhaled softly as my excess energy was syphoned. I could feel the draining of it throughout my body, but it wasn't an unpleasant sensation—more like taking a warm bath, relaxing all my muscles and removing all my pent-up tension.

Eventually the sensation faded, and I looked around me. A thin, shimmering globe surrounded us, making me feel like I was standing in a large bubble. Tejus stepped back, releasing me.

"Thank you."

"You're welcome," I replied, suddenly feeling awkward. "Should we start a fire or something?" Now that my adrenaline had faded, I was starting to feel the cold.

Tejus removed his robe and wrapped it around me before I could protest. "Wear this. I need to check on the bird—then I'll make one."

I pulled the robe tighter around me, feeling guilty for leaving him in just a shirt.

The bird lay on the grass, enclosed in the bubble with us. Tejus went over to kneel by its head, murmuring and stroking its feathers. I could see that it was still breathing, but its chest fluttered erratically and the wings drawn up about its body were almost completely white with icy frost.

Not knowing what to do, I started looking for dead branches and other things we could burn for a fire. There was a fair amount of it, and I placed it all in a pile by the bird for Tejus to light. I had no matches, so I hoped that he had come prepared or had another sentry trick up his sleeve I was unfamiliar with.

"Hazel, come." He beckoned me over to the bird. The creature turned its beady eye toward me as I approached.

"Sit by the breast, it will warm you."

The bird tilted on its side with a sigh, exposing its soft downy feathers for me to lie against. Very slowly, I moved closer, nervously bending down on the grass next to it.

"She won't hurt you," Tejus coaxed.

"It's a she?" I asked. I'd never thought about the vulture in any other way than a terrifying method of transport. Earlier today I'd risked stroking it, but the bird had hedged away, probably sensing my unease.

"It's a she. I... I call her Aria."

"How long have you had her?" I asked, tentatively leaning my back against the feathers. They were soft and warm.

"Since I was little. It's a rite of passage in Hellswan. We, my brothers and I, were all given one—it was our first-mind control test. Obviously you don't ride them at that age. They're only just hatched. You teach them to fetch things, use them as messenger birds." Tejus continued to stroke the bird, and it cooed at him.

I relaxed into the feathers of the bird, hoping that Tejus would join me. Instead he rose and walked toward the fire.

"Can you light it?" I asked.

"Of course," he replied, sounding faintly amused.

I watched eagerly for a sentry trick, but all he did was produce a box of matches and strike one of them on the bottom of his boot.

Oh.

When the fire was roaring, he rose and came to sit down beside me. Immediately I felt the heat emanating from his body, and I shifted closer to him, our arms touching.

We sat in silence for a while, watching the flames flicker around us and swirls of icy snow batter against the barrier. Tejus had created a small hole at the top of the bubble and the smoke from the fire drifted out in one thin funnel, as if it was being guided by an invisible chimney. With the crackling of the wood and the heat from both the bird and Tejus, I felt cozy—and though we were on Ghouls' Ridge, surrounded by ice flames, in a dimension far from home, in that moment there was nowhere I'd rather have been.

"It's one of the apocalyptic signs, isn't it?" I asked, breaking the silence.

"Yes. I think it is."

"So that's two down, one more to go." I sighed, wondering what would be coming *after* the signs.

"The pestilence of silence," Tejus replied. "And then…who knows."

"We're running out of time, aren't we?" I asked.

Tejus didn't say anything. He didn't need to.

"I apologize for putting you in danger yet again," Tejus murmured. "I would do anything for it not to be this way."

Smiling into the flames of the fire, I leaned my head against his bicep.

"It's not *entirely* your fault."

"I beg to differ," he muttered.

"My family work to protect humans from the supernatural. They're often in danger. When I was little, I didn't know if my mom and dad would always come home from an assignment, or if my grandparents, or uncle, or any one of them would die fighting for a fairer world. I don't mind being in danger—I mind being *alone* and in danger… Whenever you're with me, I feel okay. Like it doesn't matter what we face, because I know you'll do your best to protect me. And that's all I can ask of anyone."

"You should ask for a lot more than that, Hazel… You deserve more than that."

"But you can't give me more than that, can you?" I asked softly.

Tejus looked down at me, his expression unreadable.

"No."

I nodded, fighting down the lump in my throat. Every

time I thought that things were changing between Tejus and me, that we were growing closer, he would knock me back again and I wasn't sure how much longer I could handle it without cracking up completely.

As if sensing my frustration, he reached down to find my hand. Part of me wanted to jerk my hand back, but it would have been childish and stupid—and dishonest. I needed him, his solid presence and whatever convoluted feelings he had for me. Our fingers entwined, and I held on tightly.

RUBY

"Put me down!" I roared, struggling in the grip of Commander Varga as the bull-horse cantered across uneven grassland.

"I'm afraid I can't do that," he replied tersely, his eyes fixed on the horizon.

"I need to get to Hazel! Where are you taking me?"

"Far away from Hellswan—it's not safe."

He didn't halt the horse or stop the ferocious pace we were riding at. I could still see the blue-white flames running across the forests behind us, but we were staying ahead, outpacing the danger.

"Please stop!" I tried again. "I need to get to the castle—I need to start looking for Benedict and Julian…"

"I'm not letting that happen. You'll die, Ruby. Hellswan is no place for you right now."

I wanted to protest more. It might not be the best place for me, but Hazel was there, and so were a bunch of scared kids. I couldn't abandon them again. Avoiding making eye contact with Varga, I kept my gaze on the landscape—we were getting further away from the fires, but my surroundings had started to look unfamiliar.

"Are you taking me back to the Seraq kingdom?" I asked. I'd been assuming that was where we'd been heading, but I didn't recognize the route.

"No," he replied firmly. "I'm taking you to another kingdom. It's ruled by King Memenion—he's a fair man, he'll offer you sanctuary while the fires last."

"What?" I exploded. "I don't know him! You can't just take me to a foreign kingdom full of sentries!"

Commander Varga laughed.

"He's not like the others—you'll be safe. I promise you."

Oh, sure.

"Okay, I don't know you, so I'm not really in a position to trust you. Plus, you've basically just kidnapped me."

"Or saved your life," he replied amicably.

"I didn't want to be saved."

He didn't reply, and I glanced at him, only to see an amused smirk playing on his lips.

"We're almost there," he replied. "You might want to at least pretend to be gracious when we arrive."

I huffed silently, gazing at the approaching castle. It was smaller than the one at Hellswan, but much more inviting. Where Hellswan appeared jagged and dark, with its dull-colored stone and imposing gates, Memenion's castle was squat and round, made of lighter, brighter stone that reflected the small amount of sunlight left in the Nevertide sky. At every window, plants grew and spread across the stonework, and instead of the heavy iron portcullis and stone barricades, this castle had miles of lush gardens and fountains.

Commander Varga loosened his grip on me a little when he realized I was going to behave myself. I attempted to look as presentable as possible, slightly nervous about meeting more Nevertide royalty. The ones I'd met so far hadn't exactly left a very good impression.

As we approached the castle through a broad gravel pathway, guards stood to attention outside the main doors, and then more still appeared at intervals on the stone balconies. I had assumed, from the lack of physical barricades, that this castle wasn't as hot on protection as

Hellswan was, but maybe I was mistaken.

Commander Varga stopped the bull-horse as two guards approached us.

"Are you ready?" he whispered to me. I nodded, and turned to smile winningly at the guards.

"Commander Varga," acknowledged one of the guards, and they both bowed low. I was surprised that the guard had such reverence in his tone—why would they respect a commander of a different kingdom so much?

"We have come to meet with the king. I am hoping he will offer us both sanctuary."

"Of course, Commander," the guard replied dutifully.

Varga dismounted and helped me step down from the bull-horse, then handed the reins to a stable hand who appeared out of nowhere, also bowing low when he saw Varga.

"Follow me." The guard gestured toward the opening doors of the castle.

We entered into a very large hallway, painted with beautiful bright murals of countryside scenes. Everywhere I looked, sentry servants were scurrying about, appearing and then disappearing into the multiple rooms that opened off from the hall. Everything about it was different from anything I'd come across since arriving in Nevertide—it was a million miles away from the doom and gloom of Hellswan, and completely unlike Seraq's lavish ghost kingdom.

"Wow," I whispered to Varga as we followed the guard. "This place is actually *amazing*."

He nodded. "It's considered one of the more beautiful kingdoms in Nevertide. Small, but well-run."

A lot of the female servants who passed us smiled shyly at Varga, and each time he returned a polite and courteous nod.

"Why is everyone here acting like you're a celebrity?" I hissed.

"Because I am charming," he replied, deadpan, "unlike some I could mention."

"I can be charming," I muttered.

He gave a snort, but before I could say anything more, we came to a stop in front of a set of large doors right at the end of the hallway. The guard opened them and ushered us through, closing them back behind us.

"Commander Varga, what a pleasant surprise."

A woman's voice echoed across the room. Two figures sat on a raised dais, both dressed in light blue robes. Commander Varga bowed down, and after an urging side glance from Varga, I did the same.

"King and Queen Memenion, please accept my apologies

for the intrusion," Varga said, approaching the couple.

"Not at all, Varga. We have heard about the fires at Hellswan—a sorry state of affairs," the king replied, beckoning us closer. As we approached, both of them smiled warmly, and I relaxed.

"Who is your companion?" the queen asked, her eyes lighting on me.

"This is Ruby, a human of Hellswan who assisted Ashbik in the trials," Varga replied.

"Ah!" the queen exclaimed, her bright blue eyes sparkling. "You are quite popular among my people. A pleasure to make your acquaintance, Ruby."

I smiled back, not really knowing how to address either of them or if I was meant to speak at all.

"I was seeking sanctuary for Ruby while the fires continue," Varga explained.

"Of course," the queen replied. "Ruby, you are more than welcome to take one of our guest rooms here and rest—I imagine it has been a trying time for you."

"That's very kind," I replied quickly, before Varga could speak for me again, "but I have to get back to the castle— back to my friends."

The queen looked surprised. "You must wait. From what I hear the whole of Hellswan is engulfed in bizarre ice flames!

Why not wait a while, and then Varga can escort you back?"

I hesitated. Getting some rest did sound tempting—it had been a long time since I'd had a full night's sleep, and if I really couldn't get in to Hellswan castle, then my options were limited anyway. Varga took advantage of my silence.

"Ruby, please. It is the best thing you can do right now."

All three of them were looking at me, waiting for an answer.

"Thank you—that would be… great."

The queen smiled brightly, and I felt Varga relax next to me.

"Then it is decided. I will fetch a minister to take you to your room, and then you must join us for dinner—you too, of course, Varga."

I felt relieved that he would be staying as well. I didn't know Varga in the slightest, but I felt safer having someone around who had connections to Hellswan—as strange as that was. I supposed to me, Hellswan was now familiar.

Moments later, a minister appeared and I followed her from the room, after promising the queen that I would attend the dinner later that evening. I thought it was strange, having a minister escort me – surely it was the job of a servant? Though Memenion's castle was a lot smaller than both Hellswan and the Seraq palace…perhaps they doubled here. That, or they wanted to keep a close eye on me.

We entered the main hallway again, but then took a turn which led to a staircase and then more hallways on the second floor of the castle.

"Are you tired?" the minister asked.

I was taken aback by the question. I didn't think a minister had ever asked me a direct question, let alone a question about my personal welfare.

"Uh…I'm fine, a bit tired, I suppose…long day," I rambled.

The minister smiled at me, and I noticed how gentle and soft her appearance was in comparison with the other ministers I'd come across.

"I can imagine," she replied. "The things that are happening at Hellswan…they're terrible."

I nodded, not wanting to go into detail about just how bad things were.

"How long have you worked for the Memenion kingdom?" I asked, attempting to change the subject.

"Oh, since forever. My family have lived in the kingdom for generations. I'm so grateful that they have." She glanced over at me. "We're the smallest kingdom in Nevertide, you know. But I think we are also the happiest, and the most peaceful. The kingdom as a whole tries to stay out of

Nevertide politics."

"Is King Memenion not running for emperor?' I asked, curious. I had thought that all the Nevertide royals would be desperate for that title.

The minister nodded sadly. "Yes, he is. The queen is very reluctant to have her husband take part...but he's doing it to ensure certain royals stay out of power more than anything else."

"Tejus?" I asked. "It seems the whole of Nevertide hates the Hellswan family name."

The minister looked at me with a perplexed expression.

"No," she replied, "it's Queen Trina we fear."

Oh.

I felt another pang of guilt for leaving Ash with her, alone. I was about to ask the minister why she feared Queen Trina so much when we turned a corner into another smaller hallway. I took a few steps, and then stopped dead.

"What's...what's this?" I asked, feeling sick.

The minister's gaze followed my finger, pointed at the stone tiles on the floor. Each tile was painted with a rune that I recognized all too well. It was far more artfully done, but I recognized the inverted triangle, the snake wrapped around the thick line and the setting sun. The last time I had seen it, it had been scrawled in goat's blood in a barn.

I backed away from the minister, but she just looked confused—and embarrassed.

"Please don't let it alarm you," she pleaded. "The rune is ancient history, the symbol of the Acolytes. They were an old cult that worshiped a mythical entity—they used to be heavily aligned with this kingdom."

"An old cult?" I asked sharply.

"Yes, of course, they haven't been in existence for a long time. Not for centuries."

"I've seen this symbol recently," I replied.

The minister looked genuinely shocked.

"That's impossible!" she said. "It must have been a similar rune."

I shook my head. "I know what I saw—it was the same one. If this is a symbol of the Acolytes, then they're very much active. How powerful were they, before they allegedly disbanded?" I asked.

The minister lowered her gaze to the floor, clasping her hands tightly in front of her.

"Very," she whispered.

Tejus

It was the middle of the night when I woke. I must have drifted off; the ice fires still blazed in the forests beyond, but far less violently now. I hoped that the end was in sight. The fire we'd built had gone out, and Hazel was sleeping next to me, her head resting against my arm. The feathers behind us were cold. I pressed the palm of my hand against Aria's chest. Her heart must have stopped beating a while ago.

Gently, careful not to wake her, I picked Hazel up and moved her away from the bird before placing her on the ground, still wrapped in my robe. She groaned, but didn't wake. I watched her sleep for a few moments, unable to draw myself away from her peaceful expression in the cold light of the fires. On seeing her pale skin and fragile beauty, I could finally see and believe her connection to vampires—or what I'd heard of them in stories as a child.

I moved away from her, attending to Aria. I closed the bird's eyes and stroked the soft feathers of her forehead for the last time. She had been a good creature—brave. Brave and trusting. When we were flying over the cove, the pain had been so bad the bird had wished to dive into the inferno and end her misery. But she hadn't, flying on till she could get us to safety, holding on for moments longer to warm the woman I loved. A job I couldn't do.

"Thank you, Aria. Rest now, be free." I whispered my short eulogy, realizing that I would need to burn her body—but it would have to wait until I could lower the barriers.

Hazel murmured in her sleep. I moved toward her as quietly as I could, curious as to what she might say in her dreams…if she was ever haunted by me as I was by her.

"No," she moaned, "not…Tejus, leave him alone…Tejus, don't let me go…"

What did that mean? I couldn't quite work out if I was hero or villain in whatever scenario was playing out in her head. I deliberated waking her; the moans were becoming more agitated, a frown appearing on her brow.

"No!" she cried out suddenly, sitting upright and looking

around her wildly.

"Hazel—Hazel, it's me, you're safe."

I took hold of her forearms, forcing her to look at me. A second later, I saw the fog of the nightmare fade, and she exhaled in relief.

"Tejus, I'm sorry," she gasped. "I think...I was having a nightmare."

"It's all right now," I replied gently.

She looked around at the forest and Aria at the opposite end of the boundary. Her forehead creased in confusion.

"Why can't I sleep next to the bird...Aria?" she asked.

"She passed away in the night. She was in a lot of pain—it's better this way."

"Oh." Hazel took a moment to process the information, her eyes becoming tear-filled as she glanced over at the body.

"I'm so sorry, Tejus."

I nodded. Bereavement wasn't really something I felt able to share with others, and I felt uncomfortable under her sympathetic gaze.

"I will always be grateful that she saved me from the Ghouls' Ridge drop," she murmured, looking over in the direction of the deep caverns. "Even though riding on her scared the life out of me."

I smiled, recalling the first time that Hazel had ridden her.

She'd clung on for dear life, every single muscle and sinew in her body tensed to breaking point. I remembered the first time *I'd* flown Aria—I had spent hours dipping and diving through the clouds, finally feeling free, never wanting to come back to land.

"What now?" Hazel asked.

"We wait." I shrugged. "We can't be reached by any other creature till the fires have died down. It shouldn't be much longer."

She nodded, wrapping my robe around her more tightly.

"I'll light another fire." She was starting to shiver. Without the bird for warmth, I didn't know what else I could do to keep the ice flames at bay.

Once I'd lit a fire, smaller than the last as we'd used up most of the dry branches already, I came and sat down next to her.

"How are you feeling?" I asked, studying her body to see if it was still shaking.

"Better." She smiled back at me through chattering teeth.

Putting my arms around her waist, I dragged her over to sit in front of me. It was far more intimate than I could bear, but the best way to share whatever meager body heat I had with her. She leant her head back against my chest, so small that I could basically envelop her entirely in my limbs.

"That's better." She sighed contentedly. "You're warmer than a vampire."

"Thanks."

She laughed at that, and I smiled involuntarily at the sound of it echoing across the forest.

"Will you eventually...become one?" I asked, trying to sound offhand.

"A vampire?"

"Yes, a vampire."

"I suppose so. When the time's right, I guess. I want to be able to join GASP when I'm ready, and to do that I'd need to become a supernatural. Plus, there are some seriously badass vamp qualities that I'd like to inherit."

"Like?" I prompted, assuming by her tone that 'badass' was a good thing.

"Amazing vision. Strength. Speed. Immortality..."

"You wish to live forever?" I asked quietly.

She shrugged.

"As long as everyone I love does, then it won't ever get lonely."

"That's quite a condition."

I didn't understand the desire for immortality. I had hardly hit the halfway mark of this existence, and already it wore me down. Why would anyone want to continue their lifetime past its expected term?

"Well, my parents are already vampires," she replied, "as are my grandparents and a lot of my other friends and family. I love my life in The Shade—it's so beautiful there, and we all live together, a tight-knit community...it's something I don't ever want to lose."

I gritted my teeth. Her honest answer, a careless truth to her, brought me physical pain. Clearly she desired for nothing more than the life she had been promised. Had there even been a slight hesitation, an inkling of her wanting more than what she already had, I would have taken it—clung onto it like a lifeline.

A silence stretched out between us. It grew uncomfortable, and I felt Hazel tense beneath me, as if she wanted to say something, but didn't know how to get the words out. Eventually the quiet broke her, and she spoke.

"Tejus, you said before that I should stay away from you—that nothing would ever happen between us. Are you ever going to tell me why?"

I laughed softly, impressed with her candor, but knowing that now more than ever I didn't want to give her the choice of staying here. Hazel imagined that she loved me. It wasn't enough—not when the time came for her to choose between her home and a place she despised, and the possibility that she would have to become a sentry in order to be with me if my enquiries into how I might manipulate the marriage ceremony led nowhere.

"No, I will not," I replied, as gently as I could.

"No?"

"You should really just take my word for it."

She looked up at me, smiling.

"You don't know me very well," she replied. "I'm not going to take your vague answers seriously—you know how I feel about you. I'm embarrassed about it, but there's obviously no point in hiding it. And I know you feel things for me too…so I'm going to get to the bottom of this."

"So you're not going to trust me?" I asked.

"Nope."

"Even if I tell you that sometimes, love just isn't enough?"

Her expression changed from one of light-hearted teasing to solemnity.

"No, Tejus. I don't believe that for a second."

All of a sudden, I was unaccountably angry with her. How was I supposed to keep my honor, to do the right thing, when she was being so open with her feelings? Didn't she understand that this was pure torture for me? Knowing that I could return her sentiments, happily, but if I did so I would be condemning her to a life that she didn't want.

Of course she didn't understand.

How could she? If I wanted to protect Hazel, then I was the one who would have to shoulder this alone—to prevent her from having to make a choice that she would find impossible.

"You know I'm going to carry on loving you anyway, right?" she asked.

Her words were painful to hear. I gently kissed the top of her head, inhaling her scent—I wanted to take her, here, now. I had never wanted anything so much in all my life.

"I know," was all I said.

She leaned her head back on my chest and sighed.

"You're impossible," she murmured.

I held her body tightly, knowing that I had nothing else left to say—at least, nothing that she would want to hear.

"Distract me," she said sleepily. "Tell me about the trials—what's going to happen next?"

"Well, I think the trials are going to begin as soon as possible. What they will entail, I have no idea. My father's accounts of his own trials tended to be exaggerated—I doubt there was much truth to them. I suppose it will be the same sort of thing that we saw in the kingship trials. Harder, most likely."

"I wish I could be there with you," she replied, yawning.

"And I don't really understand why they haven't just appointed someone in the meantime—I mean, if Nevertide is under such threat, wouldn't the ministers want to do that? To stop the warnings and the entity?"

"They can't. They don't have that power. The emperor has always been chosen by trial. It's an ancient law."

"Huh, more ancient laws. They're really working out well, aren't they?"

I tended to agree with her. Why Nevertide was bound by these laws was a mystery to me also, especially when it seemed like they prevented us from saving ourselves.

"Time is running out. I hope the Impartial Ministers will see that and choose swiftly."

"I hope they choose you," she replied, curling up closer against me.

"So do I."

When I next looked down at her, she had fallen fast asleep. This time, I watched over her till dawn.

RUBY

I had tried to rest, but just ended up worrying about Benedict and Julian, so eventually gave up and took a hot bath instead. It was pure heaven to finally luxuriate in a tub of hot water without a team of kids outside needing to get in. I took my time, admiring the elegant décor of the bathroom and the lack of grey stone and vulture heads adorning every available surface.

My mind drifted to the rune that I'd seen previously. I was absolutely adamant that the Acolyte cult was active in Hellswan, and as soon as I got back to the castle I would tell Tejus and Hazel. If they were responsible for the slain goat, then how many other things might they have been behind—

like the faulty disk at the trial? Without knowing what they wanted, or who they were, it was impossible to tell how powerful they were…but if they were once revered enough to have part of a palace tiled with their insignia, then my guess was very powerful indeed.

As beautiful as the castle was, I was irritated that I would be kept here until the fires cleared. Having dinner with a bunch of sentry royals at a time like this seemed frivolous and pointless. The sooner it was over and done with, the better.

With that in mind, I exited the bath and wrapped a large towel around myself, not relishing the idea that I'd have to re-wear the clothes I had.

I stepped out into the bedroom, trying to remember where I'd lazily dumped my stuff, when there was a knock on the door.

"Um…wait, not dressed!" I called out.

A laugh came from the other side of the door.

"It's Varga. I have fresh clothes for you," he called through. "I thought you might prefer that."

My hero.

"Thanks! Can you leave them outside?" I asked, not wanting Varga to see me in a towel. Had it been a female minister or a servant I didn't think I would have minded, but it felt totally inappropriate to let him see me half-naked.

"Of course," he replied, and I knew without seeing his face that he would be smirking. I rolled my eyes.

"Okay, go now."

"Gone!" he called out.

I smiled, only opening the door when I heard his retreating footsteps fade.

A silk robe and some underclothes had been left outside the door—all in the pale blue of the Memenion colors. I dried myself and then put them on, loving the feel of the clean, fine silk against my skin. When I'd finished getting dressed there was another knock on the door. This time it was the minister who had escorted me to the room. She smiled when she saw me.

"The color suits you."

"Thank you," I said, stunned again at how polite and friendly a minister was being to a 'lowly' human.

"Are you ready to go down for dinner?" she asked. "I'm to escort you if you are."

"I'm ready, thanks."

We walked back along the hallways to the ground floor of the castle, the minister pointing out bits of artwork on the walls and giving me a short history in the different phases of architecture of the castle. The original parts of the castle all hinted at Viking origins, fitting with what Hazel had told me she'd seen down at the cove, but when I mentioned the term 'Viking' the minister just looked at me oddly, referring only to 'the first sentry settlers.'

When we reached the banquet hall, Varga was waiting for me by the entrance. He held out his arm for me to take, and I did so, relieved that I would know at least one person at the dinner.

The hall was beautiful, more intimate than the one at Hellswan, with every available surface covered in candles and wild flowers, and long silk drapes hanging from the ceiling. Murals covered the walls in here too, more pastoral landscapes and floral motifs. A large table stood in the center of the room, laid out and waiting, but all the sentries were gathered at the other end, standing by the fireplace.

When Varga and I approached, the conversations halted, but only to welcome us both to the dinner. There were five ministers present, three women and two men, as well as the king and queen.

"What news of the fires?" the king asked Varga.

"An emissary came to your guards from the Hellswan kingdom only moments ago. The fires are still not dead. They are expected to last the night." Varga shook his head. "They will ravage all the crops—everything."

"More trouble at Hellswan," the king muttered. "There is always trouble at Hellswan."

"It has been the seat of the emperor for decades. Perhaps it is to be expected."

"Exactly my point! I believe Tejus's father is behind all of this somehow. He kept his kingdom isolated, shutting us all off, and now none of us know what to do, not even his own son!" the king barked out, gesturing with his goblet.

"Tejus is a great man," Varga replied calmly. "He will see us out of this mess, if given the chance."

"You put too much faith in your king," King Memenion replied. "I have no doubt he will turn out to be just as slippery as his father."

"Now, now," the queen interrupted. "Tejus is a good man—you know that, Memenion. He can't be blamed for the faults of his father."

The king grumbled something under his breath that I didn't catch, and Varga smirked.

"What of his death?" asked the queen, oblivious to her husband's comment. "Did you ever get to the bottom of his death? I was told it came as a shock to all."

Varga shook his head.

"No, your highness, we did not. There is no doubt the investigation will resume after the trials."

I felt slightly queasy at hearing Varga's prediction. Ash had believed that Tejus thought he was the one responsible, that somehow Tejus had found out about the poisoned soup, but as nothing had ever come of it, I had stopped worrying. It hadn't occurred to me that the investigation had only been put on hold temporarily.

"Let's eat," the queen announced, and everyone began to make their way to the table. Thankfully, Varga guided me to the seat next to his, and I relaxed, knowing that I wouldn't need to be an entertaining dinner guest.

The courses were brought out by servants, and I was unsurprised to find that the food here wasn't that much better than at Hellswan. Clearly the sentries didn't consider seasoning a huge priority...I briefly thought about pancakes and maple syrup, pizza, fries, milkshakes. My stomach rumbled, loudly.

Varga raised an eyebrow, but it appeared that no one else heard.

That is so embarrassing.

"Is the food to your liking?" he asked, amused.

"It's lovely," I enthused, lying through my teeth as the queen looked over to hear my answer.

"Ruby, you must tell me about the human dimension." She smiled. "I've never been...do you like it there?"

I was about to reply when the door to the banquet hall swung open, hitting the wall. I spun around to see who had entered with such force and saw a young boy, no older than fourteen or fifteen, enter the room. He was wearing a black robe with the hood pulled up.

He scowled as he saw us and stalked past the table. I looked at the queen and she paled.

"This is our son, Ronojoy." She smiled weakly. "Ronojoy, would you like to join us for dinner?"

He eyed the table and his gaze came to rest on me. His sneer intensified.

"So the rumors are true—you've invited a human to eat at our table?" he hissed at his mother. "It's an insult! I would rather starve than sit and eat with *that*."

Wow.

I glanced at Varga in confusion, but he was staring at the boy as if he were about to punch his lights out.

"How dare you!" roared his father, standing up from the table.

"Memenion—" the queen tried to interject, but he ignored her.

"Go to your room! You *will* starve if you won't learn manners. You bring this family nothing but shame!"

The boy gave me one last filthy look, and then spun on

his heel and marched out of the room.

"Ruby, I'm so sorry," mumbled the queen, clearly humiliated. "He's young…confused, I think. I just don't know what's gotten into him lately—he's out all hours, we *never* know where he is—you know, he really used to be such a lovely boy."

"It's fine," I said quickly. I didn't know what the boy's problem was, but I'd seen my fair share of teenage tantrums. He was obviously just an odd individual. More than anything I felt sorry for his parents.

After that, the king and queen returned the conversation to matters of their own kingdom, avoiding mentioning Hellswan or quizzing me on Earth. I was glad. I felt awkward: I knew I didn't belong there anyway, but the prince's outburst had just highlighted that, and I was massively relieved when the dinner came to an end.

Varga turned to me after I'd said my goodnights to the hosts. "I'll escort you back to your room."

I nodded, and followed him out.

"What the heck was that about?" I asked as soon as we were out of earshot.

"I honestly don't know," Varga replied. "Humans are a new thing to some sentries—kidnapping them from another dimension was not practiced widely until the emperor believed it would be a good idea for his sons in the trials. Ronojoy is young. He might just be reacting to the unknown, perhaps seeing you as some sort of threat."

I nodded. It seemed a fair assumption, though I couldn't help but feel there was more to it than that. His viciousness seemed so real, like I'd personally done something to him.

"Would you like to look out from the tower? We can see if the fire is dying." Varga gestured to a small door that led off the hallway to my room.

"Do you think it will be safe to leave tomorrow?" I asked as I followed him up winding stone steps. "I should really get back."

"As should I," he muttered. "Before the next disaster hits."

We entered the top of the tower, the cold air hitting us immediately. I shivered in my robe, and looked out toward Hellswan. The ice fires were still roaring, lighting up the forests so fiercely it was almost painful to look directly at them.

"I hope everyone's okay, did you see the carriage driver get out?" I asked.

"I did," Varga replied shortly.

I turned my gaze in the direction of Queen Trina's kingdom, relieved to find it untouched. "I'm glad Ash isn't there."

"Ashbik?" Varga asked. "He's assisting Queen Trina now, isn't he?"

"Yes, he's one of the ministers assisting her at the Imperial Trials."

He nodded.

"She is a powerful woman," Varga mused. "But a dangerous one."

"What do you mean?" I asked sharply. I was so tired of people telling me that she was dangerous or untrustworthy without giving me any solid reasons why. I had my own suspicions, but other than the nymphs in her castle, had failed to come up with any real evidence as to why she was such a threat—and why Ash should keep his distance.

"All I mean is that you should stay out of her way."

"Okay, but why *exactly*?" I asked again.

"I am not at liberty to say more, Ruby. Please just trust me that you shouldn't go near that woman—and if Ashbik had an ounce of sense in him, he wouldn't either."

"Well, it's too late for that," I replied, my heart sinking. I knew Ash wouldn't be coming back to Hellswan any time soon. Without evidence to support my suspicions, I had nothing left to persuade him with.

"Can you just tell me if he's in immediate danger?" I begged, not willing to let the subject drop.

"I'm sure he's not," Varga replied, but I could see the doubt in his eyes. Frustrated and angry, I turned away from him, looking back toward the Hellswan kingdom engulfed in flames.

Is there anywhere the least bit safe in this damn dimension?

I thought about Benedict and Julian lost in Nevertide. Hazel would either be going out of her mind with worry in the castle, or be in a similar position to me—waiting out the inferno.

But at least she'd be with Tejus.

Maybe I needed to change my plan.

Rose

The Shade's Council—and the core GASP leadership—was waiting in the Great Dome for my father and Ben to return. Mom had just received a phone call from them that they were back in the human dimension, and Mona had gone to fetch them. Mom was pacing up and down, her boots making a faint clipping sound on the floor that added to my general unease.

Caleb and I had expanded our search of missing persons files to the whole of Europe, after the British Isles and Scotland failed to come up with anything that resembled what happened at Murkbeech. There was so much material to get through, thousands of incidents, and with each unsolved case we'd looked into, it was near impossible to ascertain whether or not there was any kind of supernatural involvement.

"Are you okay, Rose?" River asked. She was sitting to my right, looking as anxious as I felt.

I could hardly bring myself to nod. "We haven't managed to get any more solid clues out of the humans from Murkbeech... and there's so much information to sort through. It just feels like everything's taking too long."

"Did the witches come up with anything yet?" she asked.

Corrine had made a visit to The Sanctuary to see if anyone had come across anything similar, but it hadn't proven fruitful. The incident seemed to be isolated, which made it much harder to even hazard a guess as to what we might be dealing with.

The door to the council room opened. River exhaled in relief as Ben and my dad walked through. My mom stopped pacing and swiftly embraced my father, squeezing him tight before she released him.

"Thank you all for coming." My dad addressed the room as Ben went to take a seat next to River. My dad led my mom to the head of the table, where they both sat down. "As you know," my father said, "Ben and I have been visiting Sherus in the fae empire. He seems convinced that there is... activity stirring in the supernatural dimension that is eventually going to threaten both Earth and the In-Between."

"What kind of activity?" Ibrahim asked.

"That we do not know—nor does Sherus," my father replied, his dark brows furrowing. "We are trusting his instincts. He truly believes that something powerful and dangerous is coming our way, and I doubt it is wise to ignore his conviction. We met with the rulers of all four fae kingdoms. Sherus wishes for them to align with each other, and to draw on our resources to assist them in both discovering and combating this threat."

"It sounds like the fae are getting a good deal." Lucas spoke up, his face set in a deep grimace. "What are the fae offering us? Will they help battle whatever this force is?"

After my uncle's experience with the fae, I understood his skepticism, but I couldn't share it. If there was indeed a threat looming, then we had just been given a heads-up.

"They will," my father replied. "We might one day find that we are grateful for the forewarning as well. Plus, it can only be beneficial for us to have the fae join our network of allies—we know next to nothing about the In-Between, or what creatures might lurk there besides the fae. There may well come a time in the future when the fae can be of use."

"I don't trust them," Lucas muttered, his icy blue eyes

traveling the room until they rested on Ben. Lucas raised a brow at him.

All eyes turned to my brother.

"I do," he replied to Lucas levelly. "I trust Sherus. I also share my father's opinion that we have nothing to lose here. If the threat does reveal itself to just be a figment of the imagination, then we have only benefited by creating an alliance with the fae that could be used at a later date. And if the threat is real, then we will need them."

"So what are our next steps?" Claudia asked.

"Sherus will continue to persuade the kingdoms to cooperate with one another," my father replied. "We will need to start making enquiries throughout the supernatural dimension—see if there have been any other indicators that there might be trouble coming our way."

"Okay," I spoke up. "In that case, we need to think about labor division. Obviously the missing kids are our priority, and so far, we've not made much headway."

"Of course," my father replied. "Corrine and Rose, you will head up one team. Ben and Ibrahim will head up the other. We'll touch base every six hours for updates."

The council meeting adjourned, and Caleb and I headed back with Claudia, Yuri, Ashley and Landis to an empty office in the Vale's school that we'd temporarily taken over to use as our base.

"This couldn't be happening at a worse time," I muttered to Caleb. "It feels like we're thinly stretched as it is."

"We'll get there, Rose," Caleb replied stoically.

He took my hand, and the gesture reminded me of something he often said to me: *Don't fear what-ifs*. There was no point in me panicking about the lack of developments. We just had to keep our heads down and put in the legwork.

But a few hours later, after sifting through more case files, I was back to feeling pretty hopeless. None of them mentioned the group mind-loss that we'd experienced in Murkbeech.

"This is pointless!" Claudia exploded. The little blonde vampire shot to her feet, sending papers skittering across the table and onto the floor. "There's absolutely nothing here! I can't tell if any of these disappearances are supernatural or not—there's no pattern!" She flicked through the files on her laptop at random. "Here's one about an Abigail Stevens, aged eleven, missing from her home in Plymouth. This one's Carlito Cabral, aged six, missing from school in Oeiras, Portugal. The only thing they have in common is that they're both missing!"

"Hang on," I said, "they're both coastal towns. Pick another."

"Okay…this one's from Brighton."

"That's another coastal town," I replied swiftly. "Yuri, how long would it take to put all the case files on a map?"

"About an hour at most," Yuri replied, already tapping furiously on his keyboard.

Forty minutes later, we had all the missing persons pinpointed on a map of Europe. Now we could see a better pattern.

"Okay, so the majority of activity in the last few months has been around coastal towns—all facing the North Atlantic."

"So what does that mean?" Ashley asked.

"I don't know yet. But at least we have a place to start. The boy said that these creatures came out of nowhere…and if nobody is aware of unusual activity around the portals in these areas, then perhaps they're coming from the sea?"

"It's not an impossibility," Landis murmured. "And we haven't heard of any other supernatural activity reported in those areas."

"I think we need to take a sample and try our luck," I said. "Interview at random, starting with cases that happened closest to the water, and see what we find out."

The others agreed. It wasn't exactly the breakthrough that we'd been hoping for, but it was something. Now we had to go out and hunt down some more clues…anything that could give us the slightest indication of what kind of creature we were dealing with.

HAZEL

When I woke, dawn was just creeping up over the tops of the trees. The fires seemed to have died out, leaving behind a blanket of white frost that covered everything, coating the land in a blanket of silence that was almost deafening. I felt groggy and disorientated, and looked around for Tejus.

He was standing by the edge of the forest, stroking the muzzle of a bull-horse. He had obviously removed the barriers before I woke, and called for another method of transportation. I looked over at Aria. Her body was now almost entirely frost-covered, her wings glinting in the faint morning light. I felt bad that we were just going to leave her here, but I supposed we didn't have another choice.

"Are you ready to leave?" Tejus asked, walking toward me with the bull-horse.

"I'm ready," I said, already shivering. I wanted to get back to the castle and take a bath before I could even contemplate doing much else.

"I'll get us back as quickly as I can," he replied. "You need to get warm and eat something."

I nodded, thinking about Benedict. What kind of state would he be in? Would he be as cold and hungry as I was, but with no way of getting any comfort?

"What about Benedict?" I asked softly, already half-knowing the answer.

"It has to wait, Hazel. You can't go out again like this. As soon as we're able, we'll look for him."

It wasn't what I'd wanted to hear, but I knew he was right. I just had to place a little faith in my brother—and, strangely, faith that the entity wanted him fit and well for its purposes. He couldn't steal any more stones if he was half frozen.

I swallowed. "Okay. Let's get out of here."

Tejus lifted me onto the bull-horse, and then jumped on behind me.

"What about Aria?" I asked.

"I'll send guards back for her. She'll be cremated at Hellswan," he replied gruffly.

With that, we galloped off into the forest, picking our way across the dead branches and fallen ferns that littered the makeshift pathways. I was glad our journey would be a quick one. There was a strange kind of beauty to the snow-white landscape, but it was eerie as well—as if everything in Hellswan had died overnight, and that the world was completely empty apart from Tejus and me.

Last night had been strangely amazing. Though a threat hung over us, and my thoughts were never far from my brother, Ruby or Julian, spending uninterrupted time with Tejus in a literal bubble had been so intimate I half-wished we'd never had to leave it. I'd felt so close to him, like I was finally getting some more insight into who he was, and having an actual conversation where we didn't bite each other's heads off was a novelty I wanted to experience again.

He still wouldn't answer the questions I had about why he was so reticent in allowing something more to happen between us. I had told him last night that I would get to the bottom of it, whatever his reasoning was. Perhaps I could respect his decision more if I understood it, but at the moment I had no idea why he wouldn't just let it happen, when he obviously had feelings toward me—or at least the *possibility* of feelings toward me. I found the whole thing unbelievably frustrating, and I had no reference point for any of this. In the world of fictional romance, the guy usually made his intentions clear, and it was the heroine who had misgivings. The role reversal was getting kind of insulting.

"We're a few miles from the castle. Are you still cold?" Tejus asked.

Pressed against his body, with his arms wrapped around me, I had completely forgotten the outside temperature.

"I'm fine. Just looking forward to a bath."

"Good. I don't believe I will be as fortunate. The trials will begin this morning," he mused.

"What?" I replied, stunned. "You'll go to the trials? Can't you tell them what happened? Surely they'll delay it till you can get some rest?"

Tejus snorted. "Do you honestly believe that?" he asked.

He was right. Like the ministers in Nevertide had ever cared about the wellbeing of those taking part in the trials. I remembered the faulty disk and shuddered. Though they'd been powerless to stop it, as soon as the nightmare had come to an end they'd carried on as if nothing had happened.

"Fair point. But you should try at least," I grumbled.

"Out of the question."

I sighed. If it was a trial of willpower and stubbornness, Tejus would win hands down.

As predicted, as soon as we entered the courtyard,

ministers flocked from the front doors, running down the stone steps to meet us.

"Your Highness," they cried breathlessly. "The trials begin in an hour!"

"Can't you give him some time to rest?" I snapped, ignoring Tejus's warning look.

"There is no time!" Qentos's reedy voice cut through the air. "He must depart at once!"

"I'm ready," Tejus replied, but his gaze was directed at me.

"You're insane," I muttered. I was worried. If Tejus wasn't fit for the trial, then he shouldn't be going. The kingship trials had been dangerous enough. I couldn't imagine what the imperial trials would have in store for him.

"Hazel," Tejus growled. "Go and get warm. I will be back soon, and we'll resume the search for your brother."

"Okay."

I relented, and gave him back his robe. He thanked me with a nod, and then turned his attention back to the ministers. Not knowing what else to do, I made my way across the courtyard to the castle.

I fully intended to head straight for my quarters, but it occurred to me to check on the guards who had been on the night watch. I hadn't seen any of them outside, and no update had been given to Tejus.

The castle was busy. There were ministers everywhere, and every time I passed one of them, heading in the direction of the emperor's room, their whispering would start, but nothing clear enough that I could understand what was being said. No doubt they were talking about my brother, and it made me feel uncomfortable—and angry. This was mostly all their fault, and if they thought any differently, then they were more stupid than I had originally given them credit for.

When I reached the passageway, a group of ministers and guards were huddled around the entrance. All conversations came to a halt and the guards eyed me warily.

"What's going on?" I asked, my heart thudding.

Only silence greeted me. I tried to peer around them to the opening, but my view was cut off by more guards standing directly in the doorway of the passage.

"Can someone please tell me what's going on?" I asked again, more desperately this time. I didn't like the looks they were giving me.

"It's best if you just go back to your room," one of the guards murmured. "We've got this under control."

Yeah, right.

"Someone needs to tell me what's going on," I demanded.

"Or I'm marching right back out to your king."

The guards glanced at one another.

"The guards on night watch were found drained of their energy this morning," one of them replied, his voice barely above a whisper. "They don't remember a thing."

"Has anyone checked the stones?" I asked, my voice tight.

The guard nodded. "There's another one missing."

I gulped.

The guard glanced balefully at one of the ministers.

"We were told not to tell Tejus, in order not to distract him from the trials."

I glared at the minister, who looked down at the floor. I turned on my heel and fled. Running as fast as I could down the hallways, I prayed that Tejus hadn't already left. I burst through the front doors, aware of the ministers staring at me, but I no longer cared.

"Tejus!" I called out, looking around the courtyard wildly. Then I saw him—galloping off on the bull-horse with Lithan and Qentos following behind him.

"Tejus!" I called again, running toward the portcullis.

I was too late.

I stood panting, watching as his dark figure disappeared into the distance.

TEJUS

I was the last to arrive.

All four kings and Queen Trina were already waiting under the arches of the pavilion. The Impartial Ministers raised their eyebrows as I ascended the steps, but I was in no mood to apologize or make excuses. I knew that all the royals would be desperate to hear of the latest tragedy that had befallen Hellswan, and I didn't want to give them the satisfaction.

"Thank you for joining us, King Tejus of Hellswan," one of the old ministers announced. I nodded curtly, pleased to see his brow furrow in irritation.

"We shall begin. This trial is different from the others,"

the Impartial Minister began to explain as he paced the circumference of the pavilion. "It is a trial that will test your inner resolve to compete. Each of you will undergo a test to ensure that you are worthy of a place at the imperial trials."

"Surely our trials to rule our own kingdoms were enough," King Thraxus exclaimed. "We were not informed of this."

"Peace, Thraxus," one of the ministers interjected. "It is still a trial nonetheless, and crucial to the process. Each one of you will be asked to find within yourself that which drives you to rule. You should be glad of it." He smiled. "Perhaps you will discover more about yourselves today than you could ever hope to come to understand in a lifetime."

Thraxus grumbled under his breath, but the Impartial Ministers paid no more attention.

"You will be given an elixir," one of them continued, "a derivative of the hallucinogenic *honestas*—something that you will be familiar with, Tejus of Hellswan." The minister smirked at me as my blood ran cold. I had not forgotten my earlier experience with that foul elixir—and if the truth be told, the visions I had seen in that cave haunted me still.

"The elixir will open up the deepest truth in your hearts, allowing you to see for yourselves what is contained within you. To test for yourselves whether you have what it takes."

"How is the winner determined?" King Hadalix demanded.

The Impartial Ministers smiled. Clearly they had been waiting for one of us to ask that very question.

"All will be revealed," one of them replied in a self-satisfied fashion. "All in good time."

More riddles. I didn't think I would ever understand why ministers appeared to have such difficulty with being forthright and direct. It was infuriating, making my blood boil.

Unwilling to let them see how easily they got beneath my skin, I took the vial of elixir one of the Impartial Ministers offered me. I drained it, not waiting for the others to inspect theirs. I knew what lay in wait, and the sooner I got it over with, the better.

Almost immediately the pagoda started to spin. This was different to last time, and as its effects were instantaneous, I could only hazard a guess that the elixir was much stronger. Before I could think another panicked thought, my eyelids drooped closed and I felt like I was freefalling—weightlessly dropping through the ground.

When I reopened my eyes, the world was very different.

Bright sunlight blinded me, and it took me a few moments to be able to see my surroundings. The landscape was completely barren; miles of dry sand skittered across stone, with no mountains or ridges to interrupt the horizon. I didn't recognize where I was, absolutely certain I had never been here before in my life. I wondered if I'd been transported into another dimension, but no elixir I'd ever heard of was powerful enough to accomplish that. I had to accept that this was in some part my own imagination...but even in my dreams, I'd never seen anything like this.

I looked down at myself, noticing first that my robes were gone. I was wearing nothing but a simple black cloth tied around my waist, with a scabbard hanging from my hips containing the sword of Hellswan. Relieved that I still had a weapon, I took a few steps forward, not entirely sure what direction I should be heading in.

Deciding eventually that it was unlikely to matter, I headed off in a northerly direction.

Soon I was dehydrated and my skin felt tight and scorched by a relentless sun. I had no idea how long I'd been walking for—the landscape still hadn't altered, and I had no way of knowing how far I'd traveled. The sun hadn't changed its position in the sky, as if the world I was in had been frozen in time.

Near giving up and heading back in a different direction, I finally saw a shape in the distance. I picked up my speed in a final effort, and soon the shape took on a recognizable form. It was a cave, emerging out of the earth like a gaping mouth.

I drew closer, and began to realize there was a figure standing in its entrance. It was female, and as I hurried toward her, I began to recognize familiar features.

My mother.

I stood in front of her, gasping for breath, unable to speak.

"Welcome, my son." She smiled at me, her brown eyes as kind as I'd remembered them, her jet-black hair tossed in the heat of the wind.

"It has been a long time," she continued. "And you are the man I always hoped you would become."

I rubbed my temples.

"You are a figment of my imagination," I replied stiffly.

"Perhaps. Does it matter?"

"No," I conceded. "Perhaps it does not."

She embraced me. Her form was solid, real. She even smelled the way she used to. My heart ached from the memory. After a few moments she released me, and I stood back.

"Will you tell me what I am supposed to do?" I asked.

"You are just required to listen." She smiled again. "The crown of the six kingdoms will soon be yours, if you cut out your heart and persevere…but you must know that the path was not yours to take and belongs to another. You, Tejus, are a false king—and another destiny awaits you, should you choose it."

"What do you mean?"

"Just as I said."

"More riddles!" I exhaled, furious. "Tell me, can it be mine? Can the crown be mine?"

"It is yours, if you cut out your heart and persevere," she repeated.

"I do not understand." I groaned. "My kingdom and the whole of Nevertide is in danger, and the Impartial Ministers answer me with riddles?"

"Tejus, it is not they who do this. It is just the way. The crown is yours if you are willing to pay the price, but it is great."

"I am willing to pay it."

My mother smiled sadly, nodding.

"I wish that you were not," she whispered.

I didn't understand her. Had my mother risen from her grave, I would have expected her to be proud of where I'd reached…but perhaps my memory was playing false tricks on me. I couldn't truly remember if she had approved of my father ruling Nevertide, or what she had ever wanted me to become.

She is your imagination, fool.

"What do I do now?" I asked, refocusing on my task.

"You need to bloody your sword, beloved son."

I looked around. There was nothing—no creatures, no living thing as far as the eye could see.

My mother started to laugh.

"Honorable to the last, Tejus!"

"What do you mean?"

"Me. I am your target." She smiled again, looking brightly into my eyes.

"I can't!"

What horrific test was this?

"You can and you must. It's the only way, Tejus. You said so yourself, whatever it takes."

"Not this!"

"Don't be afraid—I am already long dead."

I swallowed, hating myself as my fingers touched the pommel of my sword. How would I ever forgive myself for this? I knew it was my imagination, but would it be another moment that I would replay in my mind, time and time again, like my brother's body falling from his tower, and the departing back of Jenus? As my mother nodded encouragingly, Hazel's face entered my mind. My saving grace. Would the sound of her laughter wipe out this moment?

Before I could change my mind, I unsheathed the sword and held its tip pressed against my mother's chest.

"I love you, Tejus. I forgive you for this."

Looking away, I slid the sword into her.

* * *

I came to back at the pavilion, looking up at the eaves of the dome.

Instantly I registered the lingering effects of my desert vision—my skin still felt burnt, my mouth parched. I was back in the robes I'd been wearing, and my sword was sheathed in my scabbard. With trembling hands, I reached again for the pommel. When I drew it out, the blade was a bright red, the metallic tang of blood suddenly infiltrating the air and filling my nostrils with its scent. Was it truly the blood of my mother? Or just some trick of the hallucinogenic drug?

Don't think about it. It's done.

I looked around at the other royals. Each was groaning as they awoke, lying on the ground as I was. I slowly rose to my feet, my head dizzy and throbbing.

The first face I saw was Queen Trina's. She looked paler

than usual, her gaze transfixed on the clump of red matter clenched in her hand. It was a human heart. She looked at it for a few moments before turning away and vomiting off the edge of the pavilion.

Averting my eyes, I looked at the other kings. Each held an internal organ or a bloodied weapon—Thraxus held a sharp rock, and wept softly into his blood-stained robes. Only one, King Dellian Demzred, held nothing. I caught his eye, instantly wanting to turn away, spare him the shame of knowing that I could see his own sense of defeat and humiliation from that single glance. Privately, I thought he was the only one that had shown any real integrity...what were the ministers trying to prove, that we would kill something we loved for power? Where was the honor and glory in that?

I also didn't understand, if these were hallucinations, how we had taken fragments of them back into reality – there was nothing imagined about the blood on my blade. Were these trials and rituals so old they now had their own ancient magic?

The Impartial Ministers stepped up onto the pavilion, coming to stand in the center.

"King Demzred, you are unable to continue to take part in the imperial trials," they announced. "The rest of you have shown your willingness to compete no matter what is asked of you. Perhaps this will bring you some comfort in the days ahead."

I wasn't so sure of that. My mother's words had brought me little reassurance—my winning was possible, but her referring to me as a 'false king' hardly inspired confidence. And what of the 'price' she spoke of? Did she just mean that the trials would be difficult, or was it something more? And what other *destiny* awaited me? I wiped my sword clean in frustration, hearing the approaching steps of Lithan and Qentos behind me.

"Congratulations, my lord!" Qentos announced breathlessly.

I turned and nodded my thanks, sheathing my sword back in its scabbard, no longer wanting to look at the faint smears of blood that I couldn't remove.

"We must make haste back to the castle," Lithan informed me. "There was trouble last night."

What?

"Why did you not inform me?" I asked icily.

"The trials took priority," Lithan replied.

"Lithan, I will tell you what takes priority and what doesn't. I would strongly advise that you never make that decision for me again—do you understand?"

The man trembled, closing his eyes briefly as he nodded his understanding.

"Good."

I strode swiftly toward the bull-horses still tethered to a nearby tree, and, without waiting for my companions to join me, set off into the forest. A few moments later I could hear them approaching.

"What happened?" I asked, calmer now and willing to hear what they had to say.

"The guards last night—they were found fast asleep this morning, all of them. They'd been drained of their energy, and another stone was found missing."

"And we suspect the boy?" I asked.

"We do. Clearly the entity is using him as his vessel, though whether that is just through mind control, or a complete invasion of his body, we do not know."

Invasion of his body?

"Is that even possible?" I asked.

"We believe so. If the entity is locked into the castle, then it would have been in non-corporeal form. Somehow it's been able to entirely control another being."

It was a theory I didn't want to share with Hazel, at least not until we understood more. If her brother had been invaded by the creature, then I didn't know what his chances would be of ever being able to regain complete consciousness—if he was ever released at all.

I kicked the flanks of my bull-horse, speeding up. I had to reach her before she discovered this latest macabre development.

Damn my ministers to hell.

I reached the courtyard in record time and disembarked. I raced through the doors, the flanks of guards hastily standing back to let me pass.

"Where is Hazel, the human girl?" I growled at one standing in the main hallway.

"S-She's in the human quarters, your Highness."

I ran.

Bursting through the doors of the human quarters, I saw a group of children, Hazel standing in their midst. She turned toward me at the sound of the crashing door, her face stark white, wide-eyed and trembling.

The children moved to let me through, and I approached her slowly. She turned her gaze to the sofa, and as the last few children stood aside, I saw a human girl lying unmoving, cocooned in blankets.

"It's Yelena," Hazel whispered. "He came back to claim her."

RUBY

The next morning Varga and I were in the stables, preparing the bull-horses. Memenion had kindly offered me one of his to ride back on, and I was grateful that I wouldn't have to rely on Varga to get where I was going. My plans had changed.

"I'm going back to the Seraq kingdom," I announced once the saddles were in place.

"Have you gone mad?" Varga barked. "Were you not listening to a word I said last night?"

"I was, which is why I'm going back. I can't leave Ash there. If Queen Trina is as dangerous as you say, and I believe that she is, then I won't leave him alone there a second longer. I can't."

Varga cursed under his breath.

"You are putting your life in danger. If you knew what…" His voice trailed off.

"No! I don't know *what*," I hissed, "because you won't tell me. And so I'm going, and that's the end of it."

Varga scowled at me, leading his bull-horse out of the stable by the reins. I followed him, the horse passive and willing. I hoped it wouldn't be too difficult a journey. I had never ridden one of these by myself, and the idea didn't exactly thrill me.

"Ruby, at least let me escort you—"

"No," I replied firmly, cutting him off. "I need you to get back to Hazel and Tejus." I hesitated, not knowing how much I could truly trust Varga, but it didn't seem like I had much choice.

"Yesterday I saw some runes in the castle," I continued. "They paved the floor of the hallways that my room was on. I recognized them. It was the insignia of the Acolytes, the same one that I saw in the barn. I need you to tell Hazel what I saw, tell her that I think the cult is active again."

Varga paled, and yanked me by the arm back into the barn.

"You need to be careful mentioning them around here,"

he whispered. "The history of the Memenion family is not as they would like it."

I nodded. The minister had indicated as much last night. Varga opened his mouth to speak again, but there was a clattering by the wall of the barn, coming from the outside. Varga silenced me with a warning look, and we both hurried around to the outer wall. Looking around, I couldn't see anyone—the land behind the stables was empty and the castle quiet this early in the morning. Varga leant down and picked up a rusty hoe.

"It was nothing," I murmured, but Varga didn't look so sure. He observed our surroundings slowly, his face pensive. After a few moments he turned back to face me.

"If what you say is true, then there are dark times ahead indeed," he muttered, walking back to where the bull-horses were waiting.

"Is there nothing I can do to change your mind?" he asked again.

"No. I'm sorry. Tell Hazel I'm sorry too—I know she needs me, but I'm so worried about Ash that I can't think straight."

"You love him then?"

A moment passed between us, and I averted my gaze to the floor, my cheeks reddening slightly.

I nodded.

Varga jumped up on his horse, and I looked up. He motioned for me to do the same.

"Has anyone told you what a bossy creature you are for one so small?" he commented with a smirk.

I smirked back. *You should meet my mother.*

As we made our way to the main part of the courtyard, and I adjusted to riding the huge, muscled creature beneath me, I realized that I would be sorry to part ways with Commander Varga. He was a good man, and a charming one—I had enjoyed his company, and felt truly grateful to him for saving me from the ice fires. Had Ash not been around…well, Ash was around—and I dismissed the half-formed notion from my head.

The queen was waiting for us by the entrance to the castle.

"Commander Varga, our thoughts are with you." She smiled softly at the sentry and then turned her attention to me. "Ruby, please forgive my son for what he said last night—know that not all of us in Nevertide have such narrow-minded views."

"Of course," I replied, meaning it. The queen had showed me nothing but kindness throughout my stay, and my evening at the Memenion castle had been one of my better experiences in Nevertide.

"Thank you so much for letting me stay," I continued.

"You are always welcome here, never forget that."

Commander Varga thanked her again, and then we set off at a brisk trot out through the gardens of the kingdom.

"Ruby, listen carefully to me." Varga spoke in a low tone as we neared the main road where we would part. "If I can't dissuade you from your return to Seraq's domain, then I won't waste my breath. But please be careful. Stay away from the nymphs—"

"You know about them!" I exclaimed.

"I do. Though I am one of the few. Remember that above all Queen Trina is a pleasure seeker—frivolous and spoilt in part, deadly and vicious in another. Never, ever underestimate her."

"I won't," I replied, his words sending shivers down my spine, making me dread my return even more.

"Follow the main road, don't deviate from its path. Ride fast. Whatever you do, do not stop, not until you reach the kingdom. Find Ashbik immediately, and do your best not to be separated from him while you remain there. Don't speak to anyone of the runes you saw in the barn—not a soul, do you understand?"

"I do," I replied.

"Then go," he commanded, turning his bull-horse in the

opposite direction.

"Varga, wait!"

The horse halted, and he turned back to face me.

"I want to thank you—for everything. I won't forget it."

He nodded.

"Just go fast and stay alive. That will be thanks enough."

I tugged at the reins and the horse sped up into a trot. Soon the commander was out of sight, and so was the Memenion castle. I followed the path as Varga had instructed, feeling strangely empty and very, very afraid.

HAZEL

We had placed Yelena on one of the sofas in the human quarters, moving her limp body as carefully as we could. I sent the children away with Jenney to spend some time in the servant quarters. They were all terrified, pale and exhausted, barely able to communicate except in rasping sobs and wild accusations of monsters in the castle, monsters they thought would come and get them all.

When they had gone, I sat silently with Tejus, both of us watching Yelena's lightly fluttering chest, relieved that she was at least still breathing.

"When do you think she will wake?" I asked him, knowing that he wouldn't have much more of a clue than I did, but wanting to say something to break the silence and bring about some semblance of normality.

"I don't know. It looks like she's just in a deep sleep. I heard that the guards have already woken. The ministers are questioning them now."

I nodded, gently stroking Yelena's red hair back from her forehead.

"She's still so cold," I replied. We had covered her in blankets as best we could, but it didn't seem to be making much of a difference.

Tejus stood up, beginning to pace across the room. In a way, his movement comforted me. It was such a familiar thing; everything falling to pieces around us, and Tejus pacing up and down a room, trying to find solutions.

"How did the trials go?" I asked.

"Fine. I am still in the running."

"What happened?" I coaxed, wanting something to take my mind off Yelena and the likelihood of my brother putting her in this condition.

"Another experience with hallucination elixirs. Not pleasant, but not unmanageable."

I thought of the first time that Tejus had experienced them in the trials, and I shuddered. I hated that he had been through something similar again, and on his own.

"What did it show you this time?" I asked softly.

"Nothing. Just fantasy and riddles—nothing of any importance."

"You're lying," I replied.

"Yes. But I'm not going to tell you what I saw. Just know that I was successful, and that the trials will continue as swiftly as possible."

I nodded. There was nothing I could say that would persuade Tejus to tell me the truth when he didn't want to. I had plenty of experience with that. Perhaps it was better that I didn't know anyway; I felt like I almost didn't have any more capacity to worry about the people I loved.

I was about to fetch another blanket to put over Yelena when she groaned.

"Yelena? Can you hear me?"

She shook her head, her brow creasing in a frown. I took her hand, holding it tightly so that she might know she wasn't alone.

Her eyelids twitched as I touched her, and slowly her eyes started to open.

"She's awake," I murmured to Tejus. He was standing on the other side of the sofa, wisely keeping his distance so not to startle her. "Yelena, it's me, Hazel. How are you feeling?"

"Hazel?" she mumbled. "My head hurts."

I exhaled in relief. She was awake, and clearly her mind hadn't been damaged beyond repair.

"Do you know where you are?" I asked gently.

She looked around, then tried to sit up.

"Easy," I placated her. "Take it easy."

She nodded, shuffling up to a sitting position.

"I'm in Hellswan Castle." She sighed groggily. "I don't remember what happened," she said, beseeching me to fill in the blanks.

"Neither do we," I replied sadly. "When I got to the human quarters this morning, you were out cold. Can you remember what happened last night?"

She shook her head.

"Do...Do you think it was Benedict?" she asked.

I squeezed her hand again, unable to formulate a reply. We both knew that it probably was.

"I'm sorry I can't be more helpful," she continued. "I just...It's all blank."

"Don't worry. It's okay. I'm just so sorry I left you here. I thought you'd be safe."

"Not your fault." She tried to smile at me. "I knew he'd be back anyway—he said so."

I glanced up at Tejus. His expression was grim.

"Yelena," he asked slowly, "would you let me look into

your mind? I might be able to access memories that you can't."

Yelena had jumped at the sound of his voice, unaware that he was standing in the room. I watched as she calmed herself, but looked nervous at his suggestion.

"She's just had her energy syphoned, Tejus, I don't think that—"

"It's all right," Yelena interrupted. "I can do it. If it's going to help Benedict, then I can do it."

Once again, Yelena's bravery impressed me. I owed the little girl big time, and I hated that she had gotten so wrapped up in the entity's plans. I didn't think I'd ever come across a human who was so calm and sensible in the face of overwhelming danger. My mom would love her.

"Yelena—thank you," I whispered. "Really."

She nodded, her smile less afraid now as she waited for Tejus to begin.

"Be careful," I warned him. "Go easy on her."

"I will," he replied.

Tejus and I swapped places, Tejus sitting down on the sofa with Yelena while I paced the room, keeping an eye on the girl for any signs of distress.

It took a while, the room perfectly silent apart from the sounds of my footsteps wearing away the carpet. When the connection broke, Yelena leant her head back on the arm rest, her face even paler than it had been before.

"Yelena, are you all right?" I asked.

"Yeah, I'm fine…just a bit woozy."

"She needs to eat," I said to Tejus. "Will you send someone to fetch her food?"

He nodded, and swiftly walked out of the door to speak to the guards who were stationed outside.

"Try to get some rest," I murmured to Yelena as I saw her fighting to keep her eyes open.

"Okay," she said sleepily, her eyes closing a second later.

When Tejus came back into the room, I beckoned him into one of the empty bedrooms so as to not disturb her.

"What did you see?" I asked.

"Next to nothing. Her mind's been wiped completely. All I could see was a shadow coming toward her—human-sized, I think. Then your brother's face peering down…I can't tell if the expression was concern or something else…and then nothing. Just a blanket of darkness, and I can't break through it. I'm sorry, Hazel."

I nodded. I had known all along that Benedict would have been involved. He might still be under the power of the entity, but at least he was alive. But it also meant that my brother was completely out of it—had even part of his mind still been his, then this would never have happened.

I had to face the horrific, terrifying reality that Benedict was, at least for the time being, completely lost to me.

"We need to locate him. He might be under the influence of the entity, but if we can keep him safe, then at least he won't be able to harm himself or others."

"We can search now," Tejus agreed. "I'll get us another vulture. Meet me outside."

He looked like he wanted to say something else. Our eyes met, and I gave him a weak smile. I didn't need his reassurances—nothing he could say was going to make this situation any better. Tejus left the room.

I waited until Yelena's food had been brought up. Thankfully it was Jenney who appeared with the tray, and I left the girl in her care. I made my way to the courtyard, relieved to find Tejus ready and waiting with another bird.

"An offspring of Aria" he announced. "Are you ready?"

In reply, I lifted my arms to his shoulders and he helped me up onto the bird. He jumped on behind me, and in a matter of moments we were soaring through the gray sky back to the cove.

We landed on the sand, and Tejus helped me disembark. I immediately made my way to the temple that I'd fallen through days before, only to find the hole that I'd created in the ground completely covered up.

"Tejus—look at this!"

He walked over, eyeing the repaired hole with distaste. There were no footprints around, the ground covered with sand and dead ferns that were still frosted over—the repairs had clearly happened before the ice fires had started. I hoped that meant Benedict was safe.

"Let's go to the other entrance," Tejus suggested. "See if we can get in there."

We walked the short distance over to the doorway we'd found last time only to see that it too had been blocked off, a large slab of granite placed in the entranceway.

"He's in there," Tejus announced.

For a second I didn't understand how he knew, but then it dawned on me that he was probably using True Sight. Which meant that the seal wasn't blocked off by barriers.

"Benedict!" I called loudly against the stone. "Benedict?"

"He can hear something," Tejus murmured, "try again."

I called urgently, thumping the stone with my fists. Eventually I heard a sound coming from within.

"Hazel?" My brother's voice was weak and timid—but it was *his*.

"Benedict! Are you okay?"

"You need to go away!" he called. "It's dangerous

here…you need to go…before…"

"Before what?" I leaned my head against the stone, crying soundlessly with a mix of relief and fear.

"Before I change again! I don't know what I might do if you try to open the door—or what might be done to me. Please, Hazel, you need to leave." His voice went up an octave, and I figured that instead of divulging our plans I should just try to reassure him. I didn't know how connected the entity was to Benedict even when he wasn't fully possessed, and right now, my brother just needed someone to talk to.

"Okay, okay—we'll go, I promise. Just tell me if you have enough to eat and drink?"

"I do. I think I must have stolen food from the castle last night. I have stuff here. I'm fine, really."

I had a sudden urge to laugh. He was a million miles away from fine, and we both knew it.

"Do you know how you got into the castle?" I asked.

"The passage here…I just have to follow the stones— that's all he wants me to do. That's all the voices tell me to do. But once I get the stones, I'll be set free—they promised they would set me free."

"That's good," I cried back, my voice breaking. "That's great. I'll be waiting for you tonight, and I promise I'll never let you out of my sight again, okay?"

"You shouldn't do that!" he called back. "It's not safe. Just let me get the stones, and then this will all be over."

"Benedict, is the...creature—or the voices—with you now?" I asked.

He was silent for a moment.

"No, they're not. They'll come back later—tonight. They're strongest at night time."

"Do you know what they want apart from the stones?" I asked, and Tejus leaned in closer.

"No. Just the stones...Queen Trina said that it was a benevolent power, or something. I don't think she's right though, Hazel—I don't think it's a good creature. It gets stronger all the time...and darker."

Bile lodged in my throat. I had an urge to smack Tejus in the face. Of *course* Queen Trina was involved in this. I should have known. But more importantly, Tejus should have known—he should have known the moment she'd tried to kidnap me, and locked her somewhere where the sun wouldn't shine, just like my brother was locked up now.

That woman would be a corpse before I left Nevertide. She would never again be able to inflict the harm on another human that she had inflicted on my brother.

I exhaled slowly, trying to push aside my rage in order to

concentrate on Benedict alone.

"We'll get through this okay?" I told him, placing my palm on the stone, wishing that I could just see his face.

"I know," he replied, sounding doubtful.

"We will. It's going to be okay…Remember you're a Novak, Benedict. We get through stuff like this."

"Thanks, Hazel," he replied, and I knew that somehow, despite the hopelessness of his current situation, Benedict had somehow managed to crack a smile.

Rose

We had chosen some of the missing kids' files at random; I didn't like relying on luck one bit, but we had no other avenues left open to us. Hopefully at least one kid among the five we had picked out would be able to give us some sort of lead. If they didn't, then we would pick out another five and start again.

We had split ourselves up: Claudia and Yuri were traveling to Portugal to speak to a missing boy's mother, Corrine and Mona were off to the northwest coast of France to follow up on a missing girl, Ashley and Landis were following a lead in Guernsey, while Caleb and I were looking into the case of another missing boy in Plymouth, England.

Corrine and Mona had equipped us with umbrellas before dropping us off at our respective destinations on their way to theirs.

Once our feet hit solid ground, Caleb and I found ourselves standing in a small seaside town, opposite a row of bed-and-breakfast hotels. We were looking for the Rusty Anchor, where Maurine Grey lived with her three sons—one of whom had been missing for exactly two weeks, the same timeframe in which we suspected our kids had gone missing from Murkbeech.

It was tourist season in Plymouth. Everywhere we looked people were milling about with their families, eating ice cream, riding on the countless merry-go-rounds that fronted the sea edge, and slurping from iced sodas.

"Easy for someone to go unnoticed in this crowd," I observed to Caleb.

"No matter how unusual they might have looked," he muttered, nodding to a group of teenagers dressed up in elaborate medieval costumes—obviously they were going to some sort of fan convention or fancy-dress party.

The Rusty Anchor was the last house on the block, painted a bright pink with blue signage. It looked like a cheery, happy place, with brightly colored drapes in the windows and a neat, orderly garden out front, decorated with various seashells and wind chimes. Sitting out front on a bench to the side of the entrance was a small boy, I guessed around twelve or thirteen, who was looking moodily out to sea.

"Hello." I approached, smiling.

The boy studied Caleb and me, looking faintly surprised at our GASP uniforms. I instantly regretted not wearing civilian clothes—in this happy little seaside town, we really stuck out.

"Are you from GASP? Are you here about my brother?" he asked, his surprise turning to fascination as he studied our faces intently, no doubt looking for the key indicators of our vampirism.

"We are. We've come to speak to your mother. Is she Maurine Grey?"

"Yeah, that's her." He jumped up from the bench. "I'll go and get her." He darted indoors before I could stop him. I'd wanted to tell him to stick around. Sometimes kids made more interesting witnesses, as they tended to be more observant on the whole and less stuck in daily routines that blinded them to the goings-on around them.

"He'll stick around anyway," said Caleb with a wry grin, reading my mind.

A few moments later, a woman appeared at the door. I

could instantly tell that Maurine Grey was a typically happy-go-lucky sort of person; she was dressed in bold colors and her hair was pinned up in a neat chignon with a headscarf. Today, however, her mouth seemed unnaturally pinched, and her brown eyes tinged with red.

"Are you here about my Christopher?" she asked, her eyes earnest and desperate.

"We are," I replied. "I'm Rose and this is Caleb, we're from GASP. There were some questions we wanted to ask."

"Do you think it's supernatural, then?" she squeaked.

"We can't be sure, but there have been other circumstances where children have gone missing recently, most likely through supernatural causes, and we wanted to see if there were any similarities between the other incidents and your missing boy. Would it be okay to come in?"

Maurine hastily stood aside, opening the door wide.

"Of course! Thank you for coming all this way."

We were ushered into a large kitchen-cum-dining area—guests' leftover breakfast plates still sat on the assortment of mismatched tables.

As we sat down at one of the cleaner tables, a sharp thump came from the hallway, and then the young boy peered around the doorway.

"James!" Maurine scolded. "Pick up whatever you've

dropped and wait outside while I talk."

"Actually, would it be okay with you if he stayed? There are a couple of questions I'd like to ask him too, if you don't mind," I said.

She hesitated, and I could see the reluctance in her eyes. She obviously didn't want her son being more affected by the disappearance of his brother than he already was.

"It's nothing too intense," I persuaded her gently. "It's just that kids can be very perceptive."

She nodded. "Well, he's certainly got a story to tell…not that anyone's believed him so far. But none of my boys are liars. They're good boys, Rose."

She called her son in, and we went through the interview process with Maurine first. There wasn't a lot she could tell us that hadn't already been put in the report. However, the cold hard facts in the police report did seem to indicate a runaway. Christopher had been in trouble with the police in the past, mainly for small, stupid acts of vandalism. The way his mother told it leant away from that conclusion. Christopher might have been high-spirited, but she didn't for a second believe that he'd left home of his own volition.

"What do you think, James?" I asked when Maurine had finished her account.

"I think my brother was taken," he replied stoically. "We

were going to see *Zombie Death House* at the cinema the night he went missing. There is no way he would have missed out on that—not in a million, trillion years."

Inwardly I sighed. Thanks to Benedict, I knew teenage boys fairly well. If the police had heard that information and taken it seriously, then they would have reconsidered their approach—that fact alone suggested that this was an abduction and not voluntary. Still, I couldn't jump to conclusions, not yet.

"And did you see anything unusual or out of the ordinary the night that Christopher went missing? Did he say anything to you?"

Maurine looked down at her hands while James nodded with a solemn expression.

"I did. I saw massive, huge birds in the sky, about the same size as a one-man speedboat. I'll show you—wait a second!" He jumped up from his seat and rushed out of the room again. I heard him thump up the stairs, and a few moments later stampede back down them again, clutching a kid's encyclopedia. He already had it open, and shoved the book in front of Caleb and I. On the left-hand page was a large picture of a vulture.

"I swear this is what I saw—because it had that weird beak and those funny legs."

I glanced at Caleb, who was studying the image intently.

"Are you sure this is what you saw?" he asked.

"I'm not totally, totally sure, but I definitely saw birds—three of them. Before Chris went missing. He had gone to the chip shop with his mates, and was going to pick me up afterward by the doughnut shop, but he never came."

"Other than their size, did you notice anything unusual about the birds, like human faces or other human body parts?" I asked. Maurine looked absolutely horrified.

"Like the Hawks?" the boy asked.

"Exactly," I said.

"No, these weren't Hawks or Harpies. I thought they might be, at first, but they were different—just birds."

"Do you have any idea where they might have come from?" I asked, knowing it was a long shot.

The boy shrugged. "I saw them come from the sea. I don't know more than that…maybe they came from miles away."

"What do *you* think?" Caleb asked, looking intently at the boy.

"I think Chris was abducted by genetically modified birds, or evil sprites that ride on the back of birds—and they came from a different dimension."

"Oh, honestly, James!" His mother rolled her eyes. "You've got some imagination."

I smiled at Maurine. It amazed me sometimes how despite the world at large knowing about supernatural creatures, some still lived in complete skepticism.

After the interview concluded, we thanked James and Maurine and then let ourselves out. Back on the busy street, Caleb and I called Corrine to inform her of what we'd learned.

"That's interesting," she mused. "We've had reports of strange bird behavior here—no one's seen anything like what your kid described, but the birds native to the area started behaving weirdly around the days of the girl's disappearance. Apparently, there was a mass migration of all species, a load of them traveling inland, away from the sea. The girl who went missing was last seen by the ocean. Her parents are convinced that she's drowned, but thankfully no one's found a body."

"A mass migration because a predator was heading their way?" I asked.

"Could be," Corrine replied. "Maybe worth speaking to a specialist. I'll get someone on it."

"Thanks. See you shortly."

I hung up, and looked around the bay.

"There should be loads of them," Caleb murmured as the penny dropped for us both. It was high season in a fishing town, and everything looked completely normal…apart from the complete absence of seagulls.

"I can't believe I didn't notice earlier," I whispered. How had we not picked up on the absence of their great honking cries as they scavenged every morsel of food in sight?

"So," I recounted, "giant birds appearing to come from the sea in both England and France—who are unlikely to be Hawks. I'd be interested to see what Ashley and Landis have to say…Guernsey's an in-between island, so if they're seeing and hearing the same thing regarding the bird population, then we need to assume that these predators are coming from a small island somewhere in Atlantic."

"Right." Caleb nodded. "We should also ask Corrine and Mona about the likelihood of a portal on an island – or in the sea. These birds are obviously coming from somewhere."

I agreed. If there was an island holding oversized birds in the ocean, then it would have been reported by now. Instead, the creatures had gone unnoticed by everyone but that small boy…which meant that they could come and go in secret. And a portal was the most efficient way to do that.

"Let's return to The Shade. We need more witches for this one—trying to locate a portal in the North Atlantic Ocean isn't going to be easy."

RUBY

I didn't let up on the pace as I traveled the single road to Queen Trina's kingdom. The forests and meadows rushed past me in a blur, and I hung on for dear life as the bull-horse's brute strength cantered along.

Part of me still wished that I was with Varga, making my way back to Hazel and Benedict and Hellswan castle. But I also knew that I couldn't live with myself if I ignored the multiple warnings I'd had about Queen Trina, and stood by doing nothing while Ash got further and further entwined in her kingdom.

Hazel would understand; she would do the same thing for Tejus—I knew she would. But it still didn't make me feel much better. I did wonder why Tejus hadn't confronted the queen. If both he and Varga were wary of her, and Trina had already crossed a line by trying to undermine Tejus in the trials, why hadn't they done more to stop her? Was it something to do with her and Tejus's romantic history? It seemed like a poor excuse to me. The only conclusion I could come to was that they were trying to avoid an all-out war between the two kingdoms…but if that was the case, then it seemed strange to me that most of the ministers seemed to remain on courteous terms with the queen, from what I'd seen at the trials.

It was baffling.

And my butt was starting to hurt. I could see the Seraq palace in the distance, and figured that I was probably okay to slow down to a trot. The bull-horse was panting heavily now anyway, and the last thing I wanted was for it to collapse on the ground, only miles from the relative safety of Ash.

I relaxed my hold on the reins as we moved at a steadier pace. My body was in agony from the ride, and I flexed my arms and hands, trying to shake out the tension. We turned a bend in the road, bringing us onto more arid land, with bushes and rocks rather than the thick forests that had surrounded me for most of the journey. It was warmer here too—the sun shone down brightly, a far cry from the gloom of Hellswan. I was starting to almost enjoy the ride when a carriage clattered up the road behind me.

Before I could start to canter again, remembering Varga's warning, the carriage was almost level with my bull-horse. I recognized the insignia on the body of the carriage—it was the same decoration as the carriage I'd ridden out of Queen Trina's kingdom.

"It appears you are back already, human." Queen Trina smiled from the window of the carriage, her copious amounts of gold jewelry gleaming in the sunlight.

Damn.

I had no idea what to do. Instinctively, I wanted to continue galloping toward the palace, racing to reach Ash, but I also knew that I had to keep the woman in the dark. Ash wouldn't just leave the kingdom on a few words of warning from Commander Varga, or the suspicions I had— he'd heard them and ignored them already. Which meant I would need to stay with him, living in the palace until I had gathered enough concrete evidence for Ash to believe me when I said she was up to no good.

"Hello, your highness." I nodded back to her, taking the decision to make polite small talk until she got bored and hurried off to her home. "I'm just visiting Ash."

"You left yesterday. I hope the fires didn't trouble you too much—terrible tragedy for the Hellswan kingdom."

"I managed to escape them. I stayed at the Memenion kingdom." I stated.

Her eyes lit up briefly, and her smile became wider.

"How *interesting*," she mused. "Though I am so very glad you've chosen to return here, Ruby. Ash has been missing you."

I wondered where Ash was. Two ministers drove the carriage, leaving Queen Trina in the compartment. I sincerely hoped he was still back in the palace, and I wouldn't be left alone when I arrived.

"Thank you, your Highness," I murmured, hoping the conversation would now come to a close.

"That creature looks rather uncomfortable to ride. They're not really made for creatures of your size, I suppose. Why not join me in here? There's plenty of space."

No, thanks.

"Thank you," I replied as graciously as I could. "But I need to stay with the horse—it doesn't belong to me. I can't just abandon it."

"Well, of course not!" she replied gaily. "One of my ministers will ride it back to the palace while you and I enjoy a more leisurely experience."

My heart sank. What could I say to that without sounding

rude and ungrateful? The last thing I wanted to do was anger Queen Trina at this stage. If she became suspicious that I was wary of her, no doubt my freedom to roam the castle would be restricted, and I'd never get to the bottom of Queen Trina's true nature.

"Okay, thanks," I replied, trying to return her smile as genuinely as I could. It was difficult.

The carriage came to a halt, and I pulled on the reins of the bull-horse. It resisted at first, huffing and snorting out of its massive nostrils, rearing away from the carriage.

I know how you feel, buddy, I thought.

Eventually the beast settled down, and one of the ministers took the reins from me as I disembarked. Queen Trina opened the door of the carriage and moved over so I could come and sit beside her. A few moments later we were off.

"You know, I find you and your companions so very fascinating." Queen Trina turned to me, her intense gaze seeking out mine.

"Do you?" I smiled weakly.

"You and Hazel in particular. Both of you seem to be very drawn to sentry men…a rather unusual development, is it not?"

"I guess I haven't really thought about it much."

This was awkward. I *really* wasn't up for a gossipy relationship chat with Queen Trina, but that was what it sounded like she was angling for.

"Ah. Perhaps it seems normal to you then?"

"Um, yes—I guess so."

She nodded slowly.

"But of course, as soon as the Nevertide border opens, you'll be wanting to get back home—back to your normal, rather ordinary lives, I suspect?" She smirked and I wanted to punch her for the thinly veiled insult.

"Yes, very much so. Back to my ordinary, boring life." I smiled brightly.

If the queen wanted to play a game of passive-aggressive, then she had picked the wrong opponent. She covered up a disgruntled frown, and I smiled all the more radiantly.

"Though of course, Ash will be *devastated*," she continued. "Apparently you have quite the powerful mental agility—you and Hazel both."

"Thank you, that's very kind of you to say."

"I must confess, I've been so desperate to experience it for myself. Every mind has a *flavor* of its own, and I imagine yours is simply delightful."

I wanted to get out of the carriage. Queen Trina's expression had gone from mock-pleasant to something far more sinister. She looked…*hungry.*

"Um, well…I don't think it's anything particularly s-special," I stuttered.

"Hmm, don't you?"

"No, Ash never thought so," I lied.

She smiled, reminding me of a wolf—the slow smirk of a predator that was toying with its prey.

She cocked her head to one side, and I screamed.

An intense burst of pain shot through my frontal lobes, like someone was dragging a blade though the inside of my skull and squeezing my brain matter till I thought my head would explode. Grey dots started to dance in front of my eyes. Queen Trina's smiling, smug face drew closer toward me, her eyes becoming larger till the deep caverns of her pupils were all that I could see. The blackness of them consumed me, swallowing my entire being until I was floating in a huge abyss, and then finally even that started to fade from view.

* * *

I woke up in darkness. As my eyes adjusted to the dim light, I shuffled backward. The gloating figure of Queen Trina stood behind bars.

"I'm glad you're awake for this," she announced. "It's so

boring making someone suffer but not being able to see their pain for yourself. Sadly, as queen, that is so often the way. One must keep up appearances, you see—and so often I have to send other, more lowly beings to do my work."

"Where am I?" I rasped, my mind still reeling from the pain that she'd inflicted on it—and I still couldn't quite understand my surroundings, other than everything felt damp and cold.

"You're where you wanted to be—in my palace. You're just not in the more lavish of my guest suites." She laughed at her own joke, and I glanced around again, fighting off an intense nausea. The ground beneath me was hard stone, and as my eyes grew accustomed to the gloom, I could make out how small the room was.

Idiot—it's not a room, it's a cell.

The bars in front of the queen…the dampness… she had locked me up in a dungeon somewhere. I started to scream Ash's name.

"Now, now," she cajoled, "he won't be able to hear you when you're down here. I've also put a border up, so there will be no reaching out with your mind…and might I add, what a truly delicious mind it was. Ash is no fool, is he?"

"What do you want?" I asked dully. Shouting had been a bad idea—my head was now thumping painfully.

"Various things. Wonderful things... but from you? Absolutely nothing. I just want you out of my way. You know, you really shouldn't have come back here. I was actually willing to let you go. But honestly, I can't have someone snooping about my castle, enquiring about nymphs and the way I conduct my business. It's so *very* tedious. And I do need Ash to help me with the trials. After that, who knows?"

"What are you going to do with him?"

Oh, please don't hurt him. Please.

Queen Trina shrugged gracefully. "Well, like I said— nothing while the imperial trials are taking place. He is rather a valuable resource. But he is a rather simple creature in certain respects, rather too puritan for my tastes...I can't imagine him faring well in my domain on a permanent basis."

I thought how ironic it was that both the queen and I wanted Ash's stay to be short-lived.

"And me? What are you going to do to me?" I dared ask.

"Good question. Unfortunately, I am unable to use you for the trials—it's forbidden to have human help, and sadly the Impartial Ministers are watching me quite closely. However, a short little syphon here and there won't be noticed. No doubt Tejus will be doing the same thing with

Hazel. So you can look forward to that over the next few days, and after that, I suppose I'll just let you starve."

I wasn't going to give her the satisfaction of seeing my fear. I nodded slowly, and then turned my eyes away from her to look at the floor. If Trina was the type who took pleasure in pain, and clearly she was, then the more resigned and indifferent I could appear, the more frustrated she would get. That would have to suffice as my revenge for the moment, before I could come up with a better plan.

She laughed again, unbothered by my attitude for now. But it wouldn't last—she would get angry soon, and angry people made errors. I would just have to be patient, and try somehow to bear the pain of her syphoning as best as I could.

I heard her footsteps retreating, and finally looked up and around at my cell. It was impossibly small, with a hole in the ground for waste, but no water or bedding.

Great.

It was like being back in Jenus' cellar. I had to remind myself that we'd gotten out of that mess, and so the same could be done here.

My best, and possibly only, chance rested in either Hazel or Commander Varga communicating with Ash. Once they all realized that I was missing, it wouldn't take Commander Varga long to work out what had happened to me—he seemed to be the only one, possibly with the exception of Hazel, who was willing to recognize the true nature of Queen Trina. They would find me eventually. Hopefully it would come sooner rather than later. Each day that passed, Ash would be in greater and greater danger as the sell-by date of his usefulness to the queen drew closer.

HAZEL

Night had fallen, and we were waiting by the passageway for Benedict to emerge once again. This time we weren't taking any chances: Tejus had doubled the guards, and we had five ministers with us as well, all ready to prevent Benedict from leaving the castle once he'd entered.

The hallway was crowded, and I moved away from the entrance temporarily to get some breathing space. I was still irritated with Tejus; when Benedict had mentioned that Queen Trina was the one who had encouraged him to continue listening to the entity, I had gotten angry. I had known all along that she was bad news, but Tejus had let her off the hook time and time again. Was it because he still had feelings for the woman? I wasn't sure. When I'd overheard them talking in the castle gardens, it seemed like any romantic involvement was in the past—but not exposing her as my kidnapper, and allowing her to continue vocally supporting Ash in the trials and *then* not saying anything when she participated in the imperial trials, suggested that he was still loyal to her, at least to some extent.

Yelena and Jenney stepped out from one of the doorways in the hallway. They glanced at the group of guards and ministers around the passageway warily, but when Yelena's eyes lighted on me, they approached.

"What are you doing? You should still be in bed," I said to Yelena. I didn't want her here to see this—she shouldn't be exposed to my brother under possession again. The entity clearly saw her as some kind of energy bag, and I didn't want her getting hurt.

"I'm going back in a minute. I just wanted to see if you needed anything," she replied.

"No, it's okay. I spoke to Benedict today, in the Viking graveyard. He's trapped in a temple there. But he was *him*, and it was…difficult. He doesn't remember what he did to you. I think that's probably best for now."

Yelena nodded. "Of course. I don't think I ever want him to know what happened. It wasn't his fault anyway."

I smiled gratefully at her.

"Have you heard from Ash or Ruby?" I asked Jenney.

"No. I think they're still at the Seraq palace."

I had thought that as soon as Ruby heard that Benedict was in trouble she would return, and if I was perfectly honest, I felt slightly abandoned by her. I also wanted her away from that kingdom… I couldn't help feeling that Ruby was in the clutches of the enemy, and I didn't like it.

The girls stayed and waited with me for a bit, giving me updates on how the rest of the kids were getting on. I couldn't concentrate on a word either of them were saying, but I appreciated the attempt to distract me. Worrying about Benedict was driving me insane, and I hoped he'd hurry up and come through the passageway so that we could end this once and for all.

I heard the shuffling of ministers and guards behind me and turned around to see Tejus making his way to where we stood. As angry as I was with him, his tall, imposing figure and implacable expression made me feel comforted despite the circumstances. If there was anyone in this forsaken dimension who was going to be able to help me get my brother back, it was him.

"We should all try our best to remain out of sight when Benedict comes through the passage. We don't know how lucid or fully aware he or the entity is; if we stay out of sight we may be able to follow him," Tejus remarked, looking down at me with a watchful gaze like he expected me to explode any minute.

"You shouldn't do that," Yelena whispered. "You shouldn't follow him."

"I have a feeling that if Benedict is coming into the castle, then there's another set of stones somewhere else, or the entity wouldn't bother," Tejus replied.

"You don't think he's doing it just to suck energy then?" I asked.

"I don't know—perhaps. But if there is another lock, then this is the only way we're going to find it in time."

"Okay," I agreed. "We'll follow him. But as soon as he looks like he's heading back, we need to restrain him."

Tejus nodded, and then headed back to the ministers.

"You two need to go and lock yourselves in the human quarters. Tejus is putting more guards on watch, but stay awake—don't fall asleep."

"We won't," Jenney promised. "We've also got some of the kitchen staff staying with us. That should provide extra protection."

"Good thinking." I smiled at Jenney. I was grateful she and Yelena were so resourceful—without Ruby or Julian here I felt wholly responsible for the welfare of those kids, and I was also *very* aware that so far I hadn't been doing a very good job of it.

They both left, and I turned my attention back to the sentries gathered in the hallway. Tejus had arranged them all so they were standing further along the corridor, back from the passage. If Benedict was to turn right when he entered the castle, he would see them all waiting, but I hoped that the entity had a one-track mind and would lead Benedict further into the castle—not toward the dead end of the hallway.

"Do you think this is going to work?' I asked Tejus as I made my way to the front of the group.

"I hope so. I'm hoping that even if he does see them, the entity is arrogant enough to ignore them. It's not like it's felt threatened by them in the past—it'll either just syphon energy off them and leave them sleeping, or just carry on about its business regardless."

I agreed with him. After the night when Benedict had been sucked back down the passage, the entity would have known that we were on to it—but it hadn't changed its behavior, it obviously didn't believe that we were a threat to it in anyway. The confidence of the creature unnerved me, but I also recognized that its arrogance might be the one weak spot that we could work to our advantage.

"He's coming!" one of the ministers announced. The group fell silent. I looked up at Tejus. He squeezed my shoulder in a gesture of reassurance, and then we moved to stand back from the passage.

I heard the grating of the stone block coming from within the passage as it swung shut, and then the methodical shuffle of Benedict's footsteps as he approached the hallway. I could hear the acceleration of my heartbeat as I held my breath, not daring to make a sound until he was through the door and standing in the hallway.

A few moments later, Benedict stepped out from the passage, his eyes fixed ahead on the wall opposite. I couldn't see his eyes from where I stood, but his strange upright posture and solemn, fixed expression told me that my brother wasn't present.

Nobody made a sound while Benedict stood there, still staring at the wall. As I watched, a small smile curved up at the corners of his mouth. My blood ran cold.

He knows we're here.

A few more seconds passed, and then Benedict turned away from the wall, heading toward the opposite end of the hallway from where we all stood. His steps were slow but sure, as if he knew exactly where he was headed, but was in no real hurry to get there.

I looked up at Tejus and he nodded. We followed him. Along the hallway we walked a few feet behind him, matching him step for step. The progress was slow, and I could feel my entire body trembling from the effort of holding myself back—not running and grabbing him, holding on to him till the entity left his form and my brother was once again at peace.

Without taking his eyes off my brother, Tejus reached down and took my hand in his. The grip was firm. It kept me from breaking.

Benedict walked on past empty rooms and the deserted hallways and corridors. Eventually we reached a part of the castle that I'd never been to before. The walls were barely lit by torchlight. A few dotted about kept it from complete darkness, but overall it felt unused and abandoned—the stone crumbling and the walls without any of the tapestries of vulture heads that adorned the main, habitable areas.

He started to climb a steep staircase, not dissimilar to the one that led to Tejus's quarters. I realized that we were entering one of the other towers, but I'd lost my sense of perspective along the walk and couldn't gauge which one it was.

He entered a room. It was in complete darkness except for

the moonlight that flooded though the windows. It was well-kept, furnished with the same velvet sofas and carpets of Tejus's living room. Benedict stopped for a few moments, as if waiting for something. Then, slowly, he bent down and moved aside part of the carpet. On the floor was a wooden door, flush with the stone floor. It had an iron ring in it, and Benedict pulled the door up toward him.

Tejus and I blinked as bright lights filled the room.

Another lock.

The stones danced in the strange formation that I'd seen in the passageway, looking as if they were almost alive and breathing—organisms in their own right. I watched in horror as Benedict ran his hand over the stones, then extracted one, taking it easily from its socket. As soon as he did so, he stood again, replacing the trap door.

Then he turned to face us.

Adrenaline and fear pumped around my body. My brother's eyes were completely blank, unseeing and dead. But he smiled again, slow and mocking.

Tejus pushed me behind him, and I grabbed hold of his robe to stop myself from falling. I watched in horror as Benedict lifted the stone in Tejus's direction, clasping it in his small fist. Tejus groaned, and I felt his mind enter mine, swiftly and desperately. As soon as the link was made, I could feel that Benedict was trying to drain Tejus of his energy.

"Benedict, no!" I cried out, trying to rush forward, but Tejus held me back, syphoning me harder as he tried to repel the power of the stone. I felt Tejus's pain through our connection. His mind was screaming—it felt like it was being ripped apart from within, his entire skull throbbing with intense, unrelenting waves of agony. I tried to open my mind, to push all my energy toward Tejus, but I could feel the grey, swirling gloom of exhaustion washing over me.

"Please, please, STOP!" I yelled, holding on to Tejus so that I wouldn't fall to the ground.

As Tejus's pain continued, I fought against the limits of my body and tried to stay conscious. My gaze was fixed on my brother—watching, disbelieving as he kept the stone held aloft, his face still contorted in a mocking smile.

Not knowing if it was my imagination or not, I started to hear strange whispers echo across the room. The voices seemed to slither and merge in a discordant harmony, hissing and spitting, coming from everywhere at once.

Then I heard a voice. It wasn't coming from within the room, but through the connection I held with Tejus. It had the same quality as the whispers, sounding just as inhuman, but I could just make out words being formed.

"Dost thou think thou art more powerful than I?" it

hissed, curling its vowels around Tejus's mind like dank mist. "False king, thou knowest nothing of my magic, nothing of my power! Kneel, kneel, false king, kneel down to your creator!"

"NO!" Tejus burst out, the cry tearing from his chest as he fought to repel the poison of the whispered voice.

He staggered back. Before I knew what was happening a huge blast of energy threw Tejus and I backward into the hallway. I slammed into the back of the wall, feeling as if I'd just been hit by a freight train.

Blearily I watched Benedict run past us, still holding his fist aloft.

The whispering ceased, as did the entity's power. Tejus and I fell to the floor, my back and head pounding where they had been knocked.

"Hazel! Are you all right?" Tejus groaned, staggering up by holding onto the wall. Dimly I nodded, and took his hand as he reached out to pick me up from the floor.

"We need to go after him," I gasped, trying to keep my eyes focused on something, but the walls and the castle kept spinning around me.

"One moment," he rasped. He clasped me to him, and I leant my head against his chest. I didn't know if it was providing comfort or keeping himself balanced, but I inhaled the scent of him and found a small semblance of comfort in his pounding heart.

"Let's go," he murmured, releasing me.

We set off in the direction that Benedict had headed, no doubt straight for the passage.

"We need to run if we're going to catch him," Tejus breathed. "Can you?"

I nodded, picking up the pace as we hurtled along the corridors. My body was screaming in agony, every inch of it hurting. But I knew if I stopped for even a second, I would give up, and above all I needed to stop my brother before he re-entered the passage.

When we reached the hallway, I realized we were too late.

The red and black robes of the sentries lay in a crumpled pile.

No...oh, God—please no!

I came to a halt at the passageway. It was empty. The door swung gently on its hinges. One of the sentries moaned, their eyes closed, oblivious to the world.

I had failed my brother again.

TEJUS

Hazel had cried softly all night.

I hadn't slept, not knowing what to do other than pace up and down the living room, feeling disgusted with myself for how helpless I seemed to be against the power of the entity.

I didn't trust myself to try to comfort Hazel. Not in the reckless and furious mood I was in. My lack of power left me desperate to take hers, to completely and utterly consume her, burying all that I felt in her willing, loving touch. I could not allow myself to surrender that way.

The words of the entity did not leave my mind. I turned them over and over again in my head, trying to make sense of them. What had it meant when it spoke of being my creator? Was it something I was to understand literally, or was it just the egomaniacal talk of an omnipotent, powerful force? It too had called me a *false king*, the same words used by my mother in the desert. Why? My power had been won fairly—I had taken part in the trials, proven my worth.

Except Hazel had the stone all along…

Was that the reason I was declared false? Did her borrowed power mean that my crown was undeserved? I could hardly bear to contemplate it. If that was the dark, twisted truth, and I was in fact a false king, then would I not also be a false emperor if I succeeded in the trials? And then more importantly, would a false emperor be able to read from the damned book, to hold power over the entity and the stones? If not, then I was dooming Nevertide to a fate that centuries of rulers had fought to prevent.

"Your highness, the trials are to begin soon." Lithan appeared at the doorway to my chambers.

"Prepare the birds," I replied. "The guards and ministers—have they woken yet?"

"Some have regained consciousness; the others look to follow shortly."

"And the humans?" I asked.

"Safe—the entity didn't go near them."

I dismissed him with a nod, walking to my room to

change. I would let Hazel sleep until I returned. She needed it, and I didn't know what we would next need to face to return her brother. If that was even possible.

The birds were waiting in the courtyard. I wanted to be early, to see if I could get a chance to be alone with Queen Trina Seraq. Benedict's mention of her name had surprised me. I had known for a long time that Queen Trina refused to play by the rules—that she had scant regard for her people, or anyone really who wasn't her. I knew of the nymphs, her indulgence in a variety of practices long forbidden in our land…but I had not imagined that she would go so far as to embroil herself in this. The fool. Did she even know what she was dealing with?

As I kicked my vulture up into the air and we soared up and away from the castle, I recalled Hazel's insistence that the Acolytes were active once again. I had started to believe that she was right, and I couldn't help but wonder if perhaps *they* were Trina's current pet project. If I was right, then it did not bode well for any of us.

We set down a few yards from the Pavilion. Dawn had broken over the mountains in the distance, casting a pink, reddish glow across the mists of the valleys and the dew-soaked grass. It was peaceful here, miles from my castle, as if the world had paused for a few moments before the day's pace began.

I left Lithan and Qentos to the birds, and made my way toward the pavilion. I paused as I approached, studying the foremost arch, the one I usually stood under to await the instructions of the Impartial Ministers. There was something tethered to the column. My heart started to race uncomfortably and my mouth dried.

I continued to walk forward, feeling like my legs were moving of their own accord, because there was something unsettlingly familiar about the shape tied to the pavilion— something that my brain was slow to recognize, but that my body had instinctively reacted to. I did not want to come closer. I did not want to see.

My stomach heaved.

I stood before a red cloak, wrapped in swathes around its owner who was tied with coarse rope to the Hellswan arch. Dumb in death, Commander Varga stared down at me. His throat had been slit.

I removed my sword from its sheath, cutting loose the rope that bound him. I caught his body before it slumped to the floor, and then held him in my arms for a few moments before laying him gently on the earth. His body was cold and stiff. All the life had seeped out of it, and I stared, uncomprehending, at the face that would no longer break into infuriatingly loud barks of laughter.

No.

This could not be the end for him.

I stepped back, no longer wanting to look at the form of the man who had once been my only friend. The only man on this earth I had ever truly trusted.

Where his robe had fallen onto the grass, I saw the lines of a mark, a thin trickle of blood. I had failed to notice it earlier, but as I stood back, I could see that blood had been dribbled in a deliberate and crude marking of a rune. One I had seen before. It was the same one Hazel had shown me on a scrap of parchment.

I could hear the panting breaths of Lithan and Qentos behind me. One of them inhaled, about to speak.

"*Don't,*" I commanded.

I did not want to hear what empty platitudes they wished to say. I became vaguely aware of the Impartial Ministers and the other royal members appearing at the Pavilion. As soon as they saw what was left of Varga, their mutterings fell away to silence.

One of them approached me, coming to stand by my side.

"Leave," I growled, not caring to see who it was.

"I cannot," the voice replied. It was King Memenion. I regarded him wearily, fractionally more willing to listen to what he might have to say than any of the others.

"You must know that Commander Varga dined and rested at my castle the night before last. Did you see him since?" the king enquired.

"No, not since the fires."

"He left us in the morning. He was to accompany the human girl, Ruby, to Hellswan castle."

"Have you seen her since?" I asked.

"No, I believed them both to be with you."

I nodded. Commander Varga had never made it back to the castle. I wondered where that left the human girl. Had she been slaughtered somewhere too?

"Do you recognize this?" Memenion pointed to the rune.

"The Acolytes."

He looked at me sharply.

"Then you know what is coming. I have heard whisperings that the cult had reformed, but I refused to believe it. That is not possible now."

I thought of the old temple, where Benedict was being kept. I could no longer doubt a connection between the rise of the cult and the growing strength of the entity. I had known all along that the Acolytes worshiped some great, unknown power—I had never thought it would be the entity. My father might have set the rise of the entity in motion by removing the first stone, but somehow the Acolytes were assisting its growth to power.

"We need to halt the trials!" Memenion called out to the ministers. I looked up to see them whispering among themselves, glancing back and forth from me to the body of Varga.

"Nonsense!" Queen Trina cried. Suddenly, I was roused from my shocked stupor.

I stalked toward the Pavilion, Memenion hot on my heels. Shoving the ministers aside, I headed straight for the bejeweled queen. I grabbed her by the throat, hoisting her up against one of the columns.

"Vile witch, was it you?" I bellowed in her face, our lips almost touching as I fought to restrain myself from ripping the skin off her skull.

"N-n-no Tejus...*please!*" she stammered, her hands weakly pawing at mine. My fingers tightened, squeezing the muscles of her throat and cutting off the air.

"If I find the slightest shred of evidence that this was your doing, I shall end your miserable life. It will be slow and it will be painful, and you will scream out to your entity, but it will *not* save you," I hissed in her ear.

"Tejus!" Memenion barked. "You forget yourself."

I smiled at the fear in Queen Trina's eyes, and then

released her. She fell forward, gasping for breath.

"King Tejus!" One of the Impartial Ministers addressed me. "Behave like that again and you will be disqualified from the trials, mark my words."

I nodded curtly, and muttered, "My apologies, Minister."

He stared at me, open-mouthed, before collecting himself and addressing the rest of the gathered crowd, all of whom were watching me with barely veiled disgust.

"At King Memenion's request we will halt the trials for a few hours to bury the dead. As soon as the sun sets, today's trial will reconvene. We meet at Ghouls' Ridge."

I left the Pavilion. Memenion would know where to come if he wished to mourn. I picked up the body of Varga, carrying him to my vulture. His last rites would be performed in Hellswan. He would be given the dignified ending of a man befitting his station, but Varga's true epitaph would be the drawn-out death I would deliver to his murderer.

* * *

Once the body was prepared, washed and cleansed by a select group of guards, my friend was wrapped in the flag of Hellswan, the golden vulture binding his body. His face had been completely obscured by the bronze death mask—the only thing that would remain of Commander Varga once his body succumbed to the flames of the pyre.

It was late afternoon, but the sun still hadn't ventured out. The pyre stood against a grey sky, and the whole of Hellswan looked dull and bleak. The only color was the bright red of the flag, and now even that was slowly becoming engulfed with the grey plumes of smoke from the fire beneath.

Guards and ministers populated the courtyard, and all of the castle staff. Varga had been loved by many. I saw Memenion in attendance with his wife, and felt glad that he had come. My friend would have wanted it.

Hazel stood by my side. She hadn't left me alone since I'd returned to the castle. I'd told her as plainly as I could what had happened. Expecting her to strategize a way to track down the Acolytes, I had been surprised when she'd said nothing, just embraced me, holding on for as long as I would allow it, her body warming mine in a way I found excruciatingly uncomfortable. Now she stood, her eyes fixed on the pyre, occasionally glancing in my direction.

Lithan read the last rites, the words I had heard a hundred different variants of. They sounded more pertinent when applied to Commander Varga, probably because he was the only man I had ever known who truly embodied the codes we aspired to.

"…he was honorable and brave. A soldier of Hellswan, a noble sentry of Nevertide. He served you faithfully, he pledged his life to protect those in his care. Let his spirit pass on to the next life; let him find more peace than he did in this one. He dies in freedom, unchained and unbound. Set free the spirit and the soul."

"Set free the spirit and the soul," repeated the crowd, as one.

The flames leapt up, running along the top of the pyre till Varga's body was completely obscured. Hazel's hand found mine, and she clasped it tightly.

"I'm so sorry, Tejus," she whispered.

I couldn't speak, and could only return the pressure of her hand with my own.

HAZEL

I didn't know what to say to Tejus.

I had never seen him like this. After the funeral we returned to his quarters, knowing that we needed to discuss the Acolytes in private, away from the crowd. We walked in silence, and once in the room, Tejus stood by the window, looking out across the darkening grey skies. He looked lost.

"I need to attend the trials; they are still going ahead," he murmured eventually. "I want you to stay here, in this room, and research the Acolytes. Find out whatever you can. I want to know their rituals, beliefs—anything that links to the entity."

"They're still going ahead?" I asked, astonished.

He nodded, turning to face me.

"It's important that they do. This needs to end."

"But—"

"But nothing," he snapped.

How would Tejus compete in the trials after this? He hadn't got enough sleep, he was most likely still weakened by the entity's syphoning, and now the discovery of his dead friend?

"You're not a machine, Tejus. Can't you ask them to wait at least a day?" I asked.

He smirked, but his eyes remained hollow.

"Will the entity rest? Will it be mourning too?" he asked. "I cannot rest while it grows in power, Hazel. Think of your brother—"

"I am thinking of my brother! I *need* you to win the trials so that we can free my brother and get him home!"

"I will win the trial," he replied coldly.

I slumped back on the sofa. Clearly there would be no reasoning with him. There would be no comforting him. I felt completely helpless in the face of Tejus's need to keep me at arm's length. After taking a few steps forward over the past few days, I felt like we were back to square one—Tejus shutting me out, while I was left desperate to get closer.

Perhaps I just needed to give him some space. Some time

to mourn his friend in whichever way he chose to do so.

"Okay, I'll get the books from the library. There's a couple of volumes I saw last time that will be a good starting point. Are you coming?" I asked, rising from my chair.

He nodded. We walked down to the library, passing a few ministers and guards who looked as if they were wandering aimlessly around the castle. Tejus noticed too, scowling at their retreating backs.

When we passed a third guard, he stopped.

"Tell the lieutenant to meet me in the library, now," Tejus instructed. The guard bowed low and hastened off. Tejus and I carried on, entering the high-ceilinged room that smelt of musty parchment and candle wax.

I started to hunt down the books that I could recall—with difficulty. Every single volume looked pretty much the same to me. I was in the stacks furthest from the door when I heard a knock. Tejus commanded them to enter, and I peered around the shelf to see who it was.

A huge, burly sentry stepped forward, wearing the red cloak of the guards.

"Your highness." He bowed in greeting.

"Lieutenant. Hazel will be remaining in my quarters this evening. She will be alone. I want six guards outside the entrances at all times, is that understood? There will be a barrier built and maintained outside of the room—the guards will be responsible for its upkeep. Under no circumstances are they to leave their post. I want additional guards positioned outside of the passageway, and outside the human quarters. Don't spare any of the men. All are to be in the castle tonight."

"Understood, your highness," replied the guard.

He left the room, and I came out of the stacks, buried under a pile of books. Tejus strode forward, relieving me of them.

"Is this all?" he asked.

"For now," I nodded.

We made our way back to the living quarters, and Tejus placed the books on the table.

"I'm due to leave now," he said, looking at the sky.

The sun was almost set. I hated the thought of Tejus left at the mercy of the morbid games of the Impartial Ministers.

"Do you know when you will return?" I asked quietly.

He smiled at me, and I got the impression that it was meant to offer reassurance. It did not.

"When I have won."

I sighed.

"We will go again tomorrow to the graveyard," Tejus continued. "You can speak to your brother again. But promise me one thing?"

"What?"

"Do not, for any reason, leave this room. Under any circumstances."

"But I thought you were going to have a barrier up anyway?" I asked, puzzled.

"That's not the point. Promise me anyway," he urged. "Please."

My eyebrows rose involuntarily in surprise. Tejus rarely bothered with manners when he believed that I was in danger…which seemed to be pretty much a constant state of affairs while I was in Nevertide.

"Okay, I promise I'll stay inside."

He nodded, seeming relieved.

"Will you see if Ash is there? Can you ask how Ruby is?" I continued. "I haven't heard from her at all—I thought she might send a message or something…" I trailed off, shrugging. I wished she'd get in contact just so I would know that she was all right.

Tejus's face suddenly looked as if it was set in stone.

"What?" I asked, alarmed.

"Nothing," he muttered. "It's nothing. I need to go, Hazel. Is there anything else that you need?"

I shook my head, wondering why he was behaving so

strangely all of a sudden.

Before I could say another word, he left the room, shutting and locking the door firmly behind him.

Okay.

"And be careful!" I called out after him.

I didn't have a good feeling about this.

It suddenly occurred to me that Tejus hadn't asked if he could syphon off me before the trial...*why didn't he ask?*

Why didn't you offer! I scolded myself. I knew I wasn't allowed at the trials, but it didn't mean that I couldn't help out in other ways.

Not knowing what else to do, I turned my attention to the books on the table. I wanted to find the image of the rune again—it obviously meant something specific, and if I could find the translation, it could be a way for us to understand Varga's death.

I had also started to wonder about the whispering voice that we heard in the tower. It reminded me of the Elders, the 'original' vampires who had spoken to our kind in a similar way, heard but never seen...but Elders were a thing of the past now. They'd been weakened practically to the point of extinction—partly thanks to my uncle, Ben. Besides, what would an Elder be doing in a land with no vamps? That wouldn't make any sense... though perhaps it wasn't too far-fetched to imagine that the sentries had an equivalent 'original'. In many ways they were similar to the vampire species. They just consumed pure energy, rather than blood. Maybe that was the 'entity'—the creator of the sentries or the first sentry, locked in the stones?

I flicked through the books. Nothing I'd read so far mentioned an original power, and without evidence my theory didn't really stand up to scrutiny.

Reaching for the largest volume, I pulled it toward me, determined to stop speculating and start focusing on the information we actually had.

Soon it was pitch-black outside, so cloudy and overcast that not a single star shone. I lit the candles on the table and fetched a robe from Tejus's room. I wrapped it around myself—it was so large, I could do it twice. It smelt like him, musky and manly. I inhaled deeply, glad no one was there to witness my love-struck behavior.

Get a grip.

I returned to the book. After studying the impossibly small text, cramped notes and diagrams that only seemed to talk of farming techniques, I felt my eyelids start to droop. The flickering candlelight was making me drowsy, and soon the letters were swimming and blurring on the page.

Just a little rest, I promised myself.

* * *

I must have fallen into a deep sleep. When I woke, the candles had burned down to their wick, and only the faint glow of the torches were left to fight off complete darkness. Through the fog of sleep, I realized that something had woken me—but what? I looked around the room, but could see nothing.

"Tejus?" I whispered, thinking that perhaps he'd returned while I'd slept. No, he would have woken me.

Then I heard a faint scratching at the door. It sounded as if it was coming from the bottom of the frame, and I wondered if it was mice.

"Hello?" I called, remembering with relief that there were guards out there. But no one answered me. The scratching continued, more urgent now. It sounded more like fingernails, small ones, running up and down the bottom of the wood.

"Hello? Guards?" I called again, my voice wavering slightly.

"There aren't any here."

My brother's voice sounded through the door, faint but definitely his.

"Benedict?" I gasped, hurrying to the door. I placed my

ear against the frame, my palms flat on the cool surface of the wood.

"Hazel, you need to let me in," he whimpered. "It's dark out here. You need to let me in."

I swallowed, a gnawing sickness pulling at the pit of my stomach.

"I c-can't do that…I promised Tejus I wouldn't open the door."

He went silent, and I closed my eyes.

Don't make me do this. Please, don't make me do this.

"But I'm your brother—why won't you help me?" His voice came again, low and pleading.

I took a deep, shuddering breath.

"Benedict, where are the guards?" I asked.

"They're not here. They left. They don't care about protecting you, but I do. We've always stuck together, you and me, Hazel. Mom told you to look after me. Can you imagine how upset she'd be if she knew that you'd left me?"

That's not my brother.

Benedict wouldn't manipulate me that way, not in a million years.

"You need to leave," I sobbed. I couldn't bear this. "You're not my brother. I know you're not my brother!"

"Hazel! Please—you don't know what you're saying. It's

Tejus, playing tricks…he's turned you against me. I love you, Hazel. I *am* your brother!" he wailed, the scratching on the door becoming louder.

Tears ran down my cheeks.

I turned away from the door, but was unable to leave.

"I'm going now," I whispered. "I have to go."

"Why are you being so horrible?" Benedict cried out, sounding confused and upset.

I couldn't answer him. I knew what he was—I *knew* that my brother wasn't behind the door…but at the same time, somewhere in that creature, my brother remained. I didn't know how much of him was present, if at all. But I couldn't bring myself to abandon him completely.

"I love you, Benedict," I said, addressing the empty room, repeating it softly like it was a mantra, hoping that somewhere my brother was getting the message.

"THEN OPEN THE DOOR!" The bellow made me jump out of my skin, and I scrambled away from the door. He started to bang against the wood, as if he were throwing his entire body weight against it.

Are the barriers still in place?

I didn't think they were, which meant there was only a lock standing between me and the entity. Why wasn't he blowing down the door, like he'd done earlier when we were in the tower?

The stones.

Had Benedict not been able to pick another from the lock?

"LET ME IN!"

The creature roared again. It now sounded nothing like my brother, the voice hoarse and full of rage, as if bile were streaming from its mouth. I hurried to my feet, determined to put as much space between me and the entity as possible. I thought about running up to the tower - trying to break the lock with one of the old weapons, but that would leave me even more exposed. *My old room.* I scurried to the small door of Tejus's secret room and pulled it open. I had never before been so glad to see the emerald green glow of Tejus's mind-stones.

I slammed the door shut and locked it from the inside.

Curling up into a small ball, I crept into the furthest corner and wished with all my might that Tejus would return home soon.

Tejus

We set off on the vultures once more, this time heading for Ghouls' Ridge. Lithan and Qentos didn't bother speaking to me as we saddled the birds, and I was grateful for their silence. As anxious as I was about the trials ahead, I was also determined to speak to Ash before the task got underway. I had forgotten about Hazel's friend, the one who had been with Varga. Hazel assumed she was still at the Seraq kingdom, and I hadn't dissuaded her of the notion. But if Ruby had stayed with Varga that morning, then I dreaded to think where she might now be.

When we alighted at the Ridge, I saw that the Impartial Ministers were already gathered, as were the rest of the royal contenders. I scanned the crowd for Ash and saw him standing at the periphery of the group, studying the Impartial Ministers intently.

"Some say they are immortal," I commented, following his gaze as I approached.

He glanced back at me.

"You don't believe that?" he retorted.

"No, I do not. They are just old."

He nodded, still looking speculative.

"Your human, Ruby—where is she?" I asked, getting to the point before I was ushered away for the trials.

"What do you mean?" he replied swiftly. "She is meant to be with you and Hazel in Hellswan…"

He trailed off as he saw my expression.

"Where *is* she?" he asked with gritted teeth.

"She is not at the castle," I muttered. "Memenion said she was with Varga…I do not know where she is now."

Ash's face turned whiter than usual, and he stared up at me beseechingly.

"Don't tell me you don't know," he gasped. "Don't tell me that you don't know where she is."

I turned away from him. The Impartial Ministers were calling for the trials to start.

"We will find her," I called back over my shoulder. I knew

I probably appeared indifferent to the kitchen boy, but I was not. Hazel would be devastated if anything should happen to her friend...

I looked over to Queen Trina. She smiled at me, clearly having recovered her confidence after this morning. It did not matter. I would get to the bottom of my friend's death, and if Queen Trina's name was so much as whispered in connection with it, no matter how loose the link, her smile would be removed from her face.

I smiled back at her.

The Impartial Ministers began with their speeches, and I half listened as I observed the ferocious winds that whipped up from the caverns to run across the perilous ridge. I knew that tonight's trial would not be easy—not for any of us.

"Kings and queen of Nevertide, the second trial commences. It has been designed to test your bravery, wisdom and strength against creatures long forgotten in our land. The creatures that you will encounter are mere shadows of what they once were, but remain deadly, and so we beseech you—do not underestimate them." With the warning still echoing across the cold night, the Impartial Ministers turned and headed off across the ridge.

We followed behind them in single file.

A minister passed us each a torch as we embarked on the

rocky path; it was insufficient light for such a place, and I once again wondered at the sanity of the ministers, and their dangerous, foolhardy methods of testing our worth.

The wind almost knocked me off my feet as I trudged on behind the ministers and the rest of the royals. Hazel had been right. My energy was not what it should have been. The entity had taken too much, leaving me exposed to the effects of the last few days. In truth, I was exhausted.

The gusts blew more forcefully, and the royals and ministers ahead began to lower themselves closer to the ground to better maintain their balance. We reached the other side crawling on our hands and knees like animals, clutching on to the rocks beneath our hands for dear life.

"Rise!" the Impartial Ministers called out to us as we reached the other side of the ridge. I grunted at them in disgust, swiftly growing tired of their imperious manner toward us all. I was about to curtly remind them to hold their tongues when I saw something moving in the thick mists.

I recognized it as one of the loathsome creatures that my father had made us battle in his labyrinth. Glancing to the left, I saw four more, each wailing and screeching inside mind-barriers, fixing us with dead stares that sent shivers running down my spine. They looked like dead things, long withered, leaving barely more than their skeletal form with thin tufts of hair dangling from their skulls and claws like razors. I had thought at the time of my father's test that he had taken these creatures from another dimension…yet the ministers had just insinuated that they were indigenous to this land. Other than my father's trial, I had never come across these creatures before.

"What are these abhorrent creatures?" King Memenion cried, jerking backward.

"Your enemies," the Impartial Ministers replied, staring smugly at the looks of horror and disgust prevalent on the faces before them. "Each of you will battle one of these beasts and emerge victorious to remain in the running for emperor."

That seems easy enough, I thought, recalling how Hazel and I had demolished them the last time. What had she called them? Ghouls. I might have been tired, and running on depleted energy, but as loathsome as these things were, I didn't anticipate the task would get the better of me.

"But you must battle them alone, without your sentry powers. Remember this is not a test of your skill set, but a test of your inner qualities."

What?

How would we manage to combat these creatures without mental power? They didn't even look as if they were fully solid. I was apparently not the only one enraged at the news—King Thraxus was shouting at one of the ministers, his rage betraying the fear he was trying to obscure from the rest of us.

"I do not see the point of a trial without our powers," announced Queen Trina. "And clearly I am at a disadvantage, being the only female here."

I almost laughed out loud at her dishonesty. I had seen Trina fight—in practice only, but she was deadly. As swift as a coiled cobra, she had deadly accurate aim and her viciousness was insurmountable.

"Enough!" One of the Impartial Minister jammed a staff into the ground. "The trial is not up for discussion—you will participate or be taken out of the running. The choice is yours."

"If we all refuse to take part, there will be nothing that they can do," King Thraxus countered.

"Thraxus, please," I replied wearily. "Let us begin this—I want to return to my home. These creatures are not beyond us…I promise you they are not."

Thraxus eyed me sharply, no doubt wondering how I could say that with such authority. I could see the cogs turning in his head—he was growing suspicious, believing that I had some sort of informant or had been given a heads-up on the trial.

"He is right." Memenion sighed. "Let us end this. I will take the risk in order to leave this damned place." He glanced around him, shaking off the unsettling winds and mists, more wary of the weather than the creatures caged in front of us.

"Then we shall begin," the minister responded, relieved. No one else objected.

A moment later, I felt the sensation of cold fingers reaching inside my skull.

Not again.

I hadn't realized that the ministers would syphon off our powers—I thought they only meant that we would not be permitted to use them. The power of the ministers was nothing compared to that of the entity, but even so, the syphoning was aggressive and painful. The more they persisted, the more I felt my insides begin to grow cold. The syphoning was also more targeted than I'd ever experienced, like they were specifically ferreting out my powers, finding the pockets of energy that contained my abilities. Anything that might help me in the fight against these grotesque creatures, gone.

I stumbled to my knees, feeling a wave of despair rising up within me. It felt like the Impartial Ministers had scooped out my very soul, leaving me limp and lifeless—purposeless in the dark, clinging mists of the mountain.

The ministers stood back, barricading themselves behind their own mental shield. With a flash, the boundaries that had held the ghouls vanished. It took a moment for the creatures to realize they had been freed. When they did, their eyes flashed with greed and malice, drool seeping from their mouths as they eyed their fleshy meals.

I had less than a moment to decide whether I wanted to live or die.

The bleakness within me leaned toward giving up, allowing the creatures to destroy what little of me there was left. But I thought of Hazel, waiting at the castle for me to return victorious. The ministers had taken everything within me, but they hadn't taken her.

I unsheathed my sword.

There were five ghouls, and each had begun to approach their chosen royal. Mine moved swiftly, clawed hands outstretched. They all screeched wildly—a blood-curdling sound that reverberated through the valleys and mountain.

I lunged forward with my sword level with the creature's heart, but it side-stepped quickly, missing my blade. It dashed behind me, shark-like teeth bared in a grimace as it attempted to latch onto my calf. I slashed again with my sword, bringing it down in an arc as I twisted away from the creature. It shot off again, its bony body writhing and twisting in the air as it swung around to attack again. This time I was ready for it, and as it zoomed toward me again, arms outstretched, my sword flew through the air. It sliced neatly through the brittle bone of its wrist, and the clawed hand flew from its owner. Black ichor seeped from the gaping wound, and the ghoul screeched loudly, its jaw descending and exposing more of its razor-sharp teeth. It moved to lunge for me again, but then froze.

The sounds of battle that I had been dimly aware of ceased completely, and all five ghouls began to retreat.

Have we won?

The creatures gathered together, back where they had been ensnared by the boundaries. Their eyes were full of malice—taunting, waiting. I risked a glance at Memenion and our eyes met for the briefest second, his as confused and wary as mine. All five of us readied our weapons. For a few moments all I could hear was the collective panting of us all and my own, erratic heartbeat.

They're regrouping.

The second the realization hit me, the group of ghouls all shrieked, flocking toward King Thraxus. He had been as poised and ready as the rest of us, but I could see instantly that the attack had caught him off guard. He had expected one ghoul, not all five of them. He cried out in surprise. I ran toward him.

It was too late.

The ghouls fell upon his body, knocking him backward. I heard the heavy, wet tear of flesh, and then looked away briefly as the claws dug into the contents of King Thraxus's stomach.

The next moment, mayhem ensured. The remaining contenders leapt toward the feasting ghouls. My sword came into contact with another limb, and as it reeled back in agony, Queen Trina plunged her dagger into its neck, slicing cleanly through the flesh. It rolled off, and she went to work dismembering the rest of its parts. No sooner was one dispatched than another groped at my leg, its claws catching in the leather of my boots. I kicked it, plunging my sword downward, but it was too quick, zooming away from the blade.

There were only four left, but they seemed to be everywhere at once. Another came toward me from the side. It was unexpected—I was watching the advance of another, and swung around just in time to see the creature sliced in half. Memenion smiled grimly at me.

I took the opportunity to glance over at the Impartial

Ministers. They looked terrified. Clearly something had gone very, very wrong here. They were focused on the ghouls, clearly trying to control the creatures with their minds—but it wasn't working.

Two of the ghouls were focused entirely on Queen Trina and Memenion. I plunged my sword in the back of the ghoul whose claws were in the king. It shrieked, falling back onto the ground. Together we finished the job, dismembering the body parts.

"Give us back our powers!" Memenion roared at the trembling ministers.

"You had no right!" Queen Trina screamed as she fought one of the ghouls. "End this now—give us back our powers!"

The Impartial Ministers responded with silence.

I lopped off another part of the ghoul's limb, and Memenion did the same.

No sooner had we finished I heard the bellow of King Hadalix. I spun around to see one of the ghouls right in front of me. Before I could react, its claws ripped across my chest, carving deep lacerations in my flesh.

The sensation was agonizing. Any power or energy I had left seemed to be sucked out at the ghoul's touch. My vision blurred, and I stumbled forward, sinking my sword into the ghoul and then releasing the hilt. As I came crashing toward the ground, I saw Hadalix finishing off the job I'd started.

Hazel.

Her clear eyes flickered in my vision before the grey swirls consumed me completely.

* * *

"King Tejus, King Tejus…he's not responding."

I heard the voice of a sentry, as if from a distance. My head felt like it was a million miles from my body, my mouth dry and arid. Slowly I came to. It was still dark, and the mists enveloped the Impartial Minister who was peering down at me, his eyes full of concern.

Too late for your concern, I thought bitterly as the memories of the battle with the ghouls came flooding back.

"Irresponsible! Foolhardy! Never in my life have I been at the mercy of a group of such inept…" I could hear King Memenion ranting and raving, and smiled in a wry amusement. At least he was saving me the bother—I hardly had the effort to stand, let alone unleash the anger I felt toward the ministers and their actions.

"Get out of the way!"

The Impartial Minister was knocked sideways, and Memenion's furious face appeared in my line of vision.

"Tejus, can you stand?" he asked.

I nodded.

"How many dead?" I muttered.

"Just Thraxus. Hadalix is wounded—he's already been carted off to the other side of the ridge. We need to get you out of here too."

I nodded, groaning as shards of ice seemed to penetrate my skull. Memenion offered me his arm, and I took hold of it, allowing the king's weight to ground me as I raised myself off the floor.

"Our powers?" I asked.

"Back—though yours won't be much good for a while. You need to rest," Memenion ordered.

I looked down at my chest. My shirt had been removed, and the wounds bound with its torn fabric. Blood had already soaked through them. I felt light-headed and weak, a position I couldn't afford to be in right now—not when my kingdom and the rest of Nevertide was in danger.

Memenion helped me walk back along the ridge. It was slow work, my legs wanting to give way with every step I took. I idly thought about asking Memenion to take Hazel back to his castle and keep her safe, but I quickly dismissed the idea. I didn't trust anyone to protect her other than myself, and she would not go if I asked it anyway.

Soon, Lithan and Qentos came into view. I could

practically see the panic that was running through Qentos, and I rolled my eyes, ready for his pointless clucking and fearful questions.

"Highness! Your Highness!" he squealed, wringing his hands.

"Enough," I barked out. "Silence—just ready the bird. We need to get back to the castle."

"But your highness, the Impartial Ministers are better equipped to heal—"

"The Impartial Ministers have done *enough*," I cut in. "We return to Hellswan."

I had left Hazel alone too long already.

Ruby

I was pacing again. Three steps forward, three steps backward. There was no room to do anything else, and the only way I could get rid of some of my pent-up fury was by moving about as best I could. Already I had pictured Queen Trina's death a million different ways—and when I'd run out of scenarios, I'd felt nothing but an impotent, hopeless rage.

I will get even, I vowed.

I repeated it out loud, muttering the words to myself over and over again until my throat felt too dry to continue. I hadn't shed a single tear since the queen had locked the cell. I wouldn't give her the satisfaction—whether or not she was watching.

Kicking the stones, I let a small growl of frustration escape my throat.

It wasn't just Queen Trina I was angry with. I was angry with Ash for never believing me or listening when I'd warned him away from the Seraq kingdom. I was angry with Varga for not exposing the queen for who she really was—as soon as I got out of here I was going to give him a piece of my mind. I was angry with Hazel even, for not magically appearing at the door to rescue me. She had known how dangerous the queen was…if she hadn't heard from me, why hadn't she come looking?

Because Benedict and Julian are missing too—idiot.

I sighed. I felt like I had a list of resentments a mile long and nowhere to vent them except to myself.

I kicked a stone into the barrier that was just visible between the iron bars. It shimmered lightly, the faint blue light casting a glow in the darkness.

Stupid barrier.

Stupid me.

I should never have come back here.

As I glared at the barrier, the glow seemed to become more intense. I thought it was my imagination, and blinked a few times, then turned my head away, and then back again. It was definitely glowing brighter.

I inhaled sharply, hardly daring to hope…

The barrier was changing! Suddenly it flashed, and a tearing sound echoed across the cell. I ran over, jamming my hand out between the bars. It had gone.

Oh!

I couldn't believe my luck. Was she dead? Had her powers failed her? Or was this just a cruel trick she was playing on me to get my hopes up?

I didn't have time to speculate. I needed to take the chance I'd been given while I could. With every bit of energy I could muster, I flung my mind outward, just as I had done in the trials when Ash was trying to find me. The key difference now was that he wouldn't be listening for me—so the communication channel was entirely one-sided…and I wasn't sure that it was going to work this way.

Ash! Ash—please hear me!

Nothing. I felt the impossibility of the task weighing down on me.

Don't give up! I scolded myself. Taking a deep breath, I sat down on the floor. I closed my eyes and tried to picture him, somewhere within the palace, wandering down an empty hallway.

Ash! Ash, can you hear me? It's Ruby!

Still nothing.

I tried again, focusing on the image of Ash, picturing him as clearly as I could in my mind. It wasn't hard. *Hey, shortie,* I imagined him saying, *what are you doing here?* I smiled at the thought, sending out images of gold light with my mind—imagining it traveling to reach him, wherever he was.

Then I got a reply.

It was tentative at first, like a slight breeze of energy whispering about me. But then I felt him: Ash entering my mind—fighting through the physical distance between us.

Ruby?

I heard his voice echo through my mind. I still couldn't see him, but I could feel him and hear him. It was enough.

Ash, I'm locked in a dungeon, in Queen Trina's palace—please come get me!

I pictured the cell, the bars on the door and the dank stone. I sent it outward, trying to strengthen our connection with visual memories and images. Soon I could feel rage travel back toward me—it was his rage, mixed with shame and self-loathing for not listening to me.

I tried to reassure him that it was all right, that I just wanted to get out, but his feelings were strong, and they overwhelmed the connection for a while. Then I felt a more reassuring emotion—determination. Ash was going to find me.

I kept my eyes closed, trying to focus entirely on the connection that had formed. Eventually an image flickered into my mind—it was of a carriage, one of Queen Trina's, and Ash was riding alongside it. Through the window I could see that Queen Trina looked pale and weak, being held by another minister whom she appeared to be syphoning off.

It made sense. Queen Trina had somehow been weakened in the trial, and hence the barriers had come down. I sent back my anxiety that soon she would regain full strength, and I felt Ash's response. It didn't matter now, even if her powers did come back, Ash would do whatever it took to get me out of here. I could feel his resolve strengthening our bond.

I sighed in relief.

Not wanting to leave him, I stayed a moment longer, drifting around in my mind, just wanting to feel connected to Ash in some way. I smiled as he sent through an image of him rescuing me from the palace dungeons. In it we kissed, and it was so real that I could almost feel the sensation of his lips pressed against mine.

The connection started to break, the images becoming fainter and fainter until they disappeared altogether and I was left alone in my cell once more.

It no longer bothered me as much as it had.

For the second time since arriving in Nevertide, Ash was going to come and save my ass.

Hazel

I was woken by the sound of jangling keys before a crack of light appeared in the doorway. I shrank back against the corner of the stone room, shielding my eyes with my hands and making my body as small as I possibly could.

"Hazel!" Tejus's voice splintered through my fear, and I lifted my head up in disbelief.

"Tejus?" I gulped, so grateful and relieved to see him that I wanted to cry. I crawled toward the doorway, my body aching from being cramped up for so long.

"What in Hellswan happened?"

"B-Benedict…under the control of the entity. It was awful."

It was all I could manage to say about what happened. I didn't want to relive the memory. Ever.

I stumbled out into the light of the room, and got my first proper look at Tejus.

"What happened to you?" I cried. His bare torso was covered with blood and his face ashen.

"Trials," he replied with a sardonic grin. Then he reached out to hold me at arm's length, and his expression turned painfully solemn. "Hazel, I'm so sorry I left you alone. I shouldn't have done it. It was foolish and irresponsible."

I couldn't really take in what he was saying—my gaze was entirely fixed on the blood seeping from his chest, and the taut muscles of his torso as they quivered in pain. He was covered in a thin sheen of sweat and looked feverish. What had they done to him?

"On the sofa, now," I replied sternly.

He nodded, and dropped his arms. He turned to walk slowly across the room and I could see bruises starting to form on his back, and more, shallower, cuts.

I helped him lie down, making sure there was a cushion behind his head, and removed some of the books that I'd left lying around.

"Shall I fetch the ministers?" I asked, not knowing who else was going to help heal him.

He winced. "No—I think I've had enough of the ministers for one night. I'll recover fine on my own, I just need to rest."

"Okay, but I need to clean your wounds," I replied, eyeing the unhygienic-looking shirt tatters that seemed to be holding him together. I stood up to get a bowl of hot water from the bathroom, but he grabbed my hand.

"Wait—there's something I need to tell you. It's Ruby. Ash doesn't know where she is. She was with Varga, and heading back to the palace, but she didn't arrive."

"What?" I gasped.

I tried to steady the panic that was building up inside me. If she was travelling with Varga then perhaps she was with his killers now—and in serious trouble.

"Tejus?" I swallowed, wanting him to say something that would put my mind at ease. Maybe he had a theory that was more optimistic than mine?

"We'll look for her as soon as we can." He sighed. "But I can't keep hunting down your friends like this. Can't you keep them in one place?" He managed a weak smile at his own joke, and I squeezed his hand.

"Hopefully she's okay. Ruby's pretty capable—w-we'll find her when you're better…and hopefully Ash will have enough sense to start looking for her too." I tried to reassure myself as much as Tejus. I didn't want him thinking that he needed to somehow miraculously speed up his recovery to help me and my friends once again. He had been through enough.

"I'm going to get hot water, don't move."

He cocked an eyebrow up at me in amusement as I hurried out of the room. Guards were back in position outside the door, five nodding a good morning to me, all looking shame-faced. They obviously realized that they'd failed in their job to protect me. Not their fault, obviously, but I didn't want to discuss it or pretend that everything was fine when it so blatantly wasn't.

I entered the bathroom, and while I searched for something to use as a bowl, and located some clean towels, I felt anxiety starting to consume me. I tried to push my fears for Ruby to one side. There was nothing that I could do to help her right now. To go off on my own in Nevertide felt like an irresponsible thing to do, especially with Benedict now fully possessed by the entity. If I went missing like Julian and Ruby, then who would help him?

Finding an old brass bowl that had obviously once been used to hold dried flowers, I washed it out as thoroughly as I could and then ran the hot water until it spilled out with billows of steam. I carried all of the equipment back to the living room.

"Do you have alcohol here?" I asked one of the guards.

"Umm…" He looked taken aback by the question. "Like mead?"

"No—like spirits; really strong alcohol…vodka? It's to clean a wound."

He looked puzzled, but then nodded.

"I think I know what you mean. I'll have some brought up."

"Thanks," I murmured as he opened the door to the living quarters for me.

Placing the bowl on the floor by the sofa, I looked over at Tejus. He was still conscious, but his breathing had taken on a rasping quality, as if the effort of moving his chest was becoming harder.

"What did this?" I asked, kneeling up to slowly try to remove the makeshift bandages. His skin was too hot. He winced as my colder fingers touched the swollen skin around the wounds.

"Ghouls. But they were out of control. The ministers took our powers, and we tried to fight them, but they seemed so much more alert and intelligent than the ones you and I came across in the Labyrinth…almost as if they were organizing themselves at one point. King Thraxus died."

I was speechless. It was completely barbaric! To remove the sentries' powers and put them in front of ghouls? The Impartial Ministers were insane. Surely the last trial and the faulty disk had been enough for them to learn to temper the tests that they put the contestants under? Didn't they *learn*? They were meant to be the council of Nevertide…but to me they seemed about as dumb as a bunch of hens.

I also felt a wave of relief pass through me that it wasn't Tejus who was dead. Ghouls were foul creatures, and my family had plenty of experience to support that.

"You knew what they were," Tejus murmured, "when we were in the Labyrinth…are those creatures something that your people have come across before?"

I briefly told him about my uncle Benjamin in The Underworld—kept there with thousands of other spirits like goldfish for the ghouls' amusement.

"I was surprised to see ghouls here," I remarked.

Tejus took a sharp intake of breath as I removed the last of the bloody bandages. "I thought they came from another dimension…but the ministers claimed that the ghouls have long been creatures of this land."

I wondered why they hadn't been mentioned in any of the books that I'd read of Nevertide's history. More evidence of the ministers being vague and inept? I wasn't sure. And I wondered if the sentries truly knew how dangerous and malicious the creatures were—especially if they'd been willing to let them take part in a trial. Then again, so far the ministers of Nevertide hadn't exactly shown that they valued the lives of their people very highly.

I wet the towel and placed it as gently as I could against Tejus's wounds. Now that the bandages were removed, I could see that there were four deep gashes torn into his skin. The skin around them looked faintly bluish, as if it were infected. I needed the guard to hurry up with the alcohol.

"You should really get a minister to take a look at this— or who else in Nevertide knows about healing?" I asked.

Tejus's eyes flickered open.

"We normally heal quite well on our own," he replied softly. "My energy will just take a little while longer to come back."

"You can syphon off me when this is finished," I replied. "Take as much as you need—I spent the night in the stone room, so I should be good."

"Thank you," he breathed.

The guard knocked at the door, and I hurried to get the alcohol I hoped he'd brought me. He handed it to me with the same bemused expression as he'd exhibited earlier. It was a tall glass bottle, with the liquid inside completely clear.

"Thanks."

I closed the door before he could say anything else, wondering why he thought it was so strange that I'd asked for it. Maybe sentries didn't use alcohol as a disinfectant? If they had healing properties of their own, perhaps they usually didn't need it.

"This is going to hurt," I murmured, uncorking the bottle. The smell of pure alcohol assaulted my nostrils.

Disgusting.

"What is?" he asked blearily.

"This."

I poured the liquid on his chest. Every muscle in his body seemed to jump in reflex, and he took a sharp hiss of breath before grinding his teeth.

"Ah!" he choked. "That."

I smiled. How was Tejus being so good-humored with all this? He was taciturn and grumpy normally. Did extreme pain cheer him up or something? Weirdo.

Now that his wounds were disinfected I could start removing the rest of the blood. I set about cleaning him up, making sure my touches were as light as possible. Soon the liquid in the bowl was bright red, but his chest already looked better, the blue tinge of the skin returning to Tejus's normal hue.

You can stop now, I thought.

I really didn't want to. Unrestricted access to Tejus was rare. I was having trouble containing my imagination as I wiped the towels over his six-pack and biceps. His entire body looked like it had been carved out of marble—it was hard and unyielding...but I could all too easily recall how soft and tender his touch could be.

Get a grip.

I looked away guiltily.

His eyes were closed, and his face now relaxed in sleep. I hoped that meant some of the pain had eased, but I didn't want to wake him to ask. I discarded the towel, pleased to note that the wound was no longer seeping blood. His healing powers were impressive—that type of cut should have bled for hours.

Leaning forward on my knees, I brushed a few stray strands of hair away from his forehead. Unable to help myself, I gently placed my lips over his. The kiss lasted for less than a moment, but the after-effects lingered long after that—a warm glow suffusing my body.

"Do you always kiss your patients?" His mocking voice broke the silence of the room.

I glared at Tejus, a hot flush rising in my cheeks from being caught red-handed.

"I didn't mean to wake you," I muttered.

"You didn't. I wasn't asleep."

He smirked at me, knowingly.

"Whatever," I huffed. "You should probably syphon off me now anyway."

The smile didn't leave his face, but he closed his eyes again. A moment later I could feel the pleasant tingling sensation of our mind-meld beginning. I leaned against the sofa, my body relaxing as I let Tejus take what he needed from me. We didn't share images or memories this time, just focused on the energy that was passing from my mind to his. It felt hazy and comforting, like I was drifting down a river or something, lost to the world.

Eventually the connection started to fade. I thought something was wrong, but when I looked up at Tejus, I realized he was truly asleep this time—his chest rising and falling with deep breaths.

I watched over him for a while, a tight, knotted sensation building in my chest. I cared for Tejus too much. Without me realizing it, he had slowly become just as important to me as my brother and Ruby and Julian. I worried about him, worried that I asked too much of him—it wasn't right that he was having to continually hunt down my friends, to be preoccupied with my safety while he was trying to compete in the trials. In the past I had felt that it was a fair deal—he and his brothers had brought us here, they should do everything in their power to keep us safe. As Tejus was the only one capable of doing that, the task was left to him alone. But that feeling was gone. He had more than repaid the debt.

And I loved him.

I knew he felt the same way. I knew Tejus well enough now to know that the way he treated me was completely different from how he treated all others, that he wanted me as much as I wanted him. We had a connection beyond mind-melds and the fact that we had been flung together by chance.

I just needed to persuade him to get over whatever was holding him back from allowing him to let go, to admit that we would be good for one another—that this could be so much *more*.

ASH

I had been an idiot.

Why hadn't I listened to Ruby when she'd told me how dangerous Queen Trina was? I wanted to think that it was because I'd been determined to make a difference in Nevertide, to help people like me who never got a fair chance. The truth was, it was probably a lot more to do with my pride and arrogance—wanting to rise up against the Hellswans and prove that I was more than just a kitchen boy. The *honestas* hallucinations had been right—I would stop at nothing, not even bothering to listen to the girl I was in love with when she told me I was making a mistake.

So I had put her in harm's way—and she was paying for

my mistake.

Ruby had shown me a dungeon, a dark and damp place, which I could only assume was beneath the palace somewhere. The problem was, this place was like a labyrinth: I was constantly getting lost, even though I mostly stuck to the same area of the palace—back and forth to my room, the council chamber and Queen Trina's private office.

The queen was still weak from the syphoning and the subsequent battle. She had been injured badly, and as soon as we had returned to the palace, she had locked herself in her room with two other ministers to revive her energy. I had never seen anything like last night's trial. The ministers had gone too far this time. Surely someone would tell them to stop—that the contest was becoming too dangerous. Something had gone wrong. The Impartial Ministers hadn't been prepared, just like at the disk trial. Something *else* had been controlling the show...I just didn't know what.

Right now though, trying to understand what the hell was going on in Nevertide wasn't my priority—Ruby was.

I started walking in the opposite direction from Queen Trina's chambers. I didn't know where I was heading, but I wanted to get as far into the depths of the castle as I could, as quickly as I could. The moment that Queen Trina regained her full strength, the barriers around Ruby's cell would return. There had to be a trap door or entrance somewhere to the dungeons—and I would most likely find it near storerooms or servant areas.

The palace, as usual, was deserted.

I didn't know if it was a hindrance or a help—on the one hand it meant I could explore undetected, but it also meant that I couldn't ask anyone directions to the lower levels of the building, even under the guise of an urgent request from the queen.

Passing empty, lavish courtyards and long, polished tile corridors, I started to feel more and more lost. I quickened my pace, and started using True Sight to look in all the rooms that led off from the main hallway. They were all empty save for opulent furniture, and occasionally brightly colored birds held in cages who all called out as soon as I saw them, sensing something was there.

Eventually, the opulence and polish started to fade. The grand hallway shrank, and then broke off to smaller passageways—all white-washed stone, but without any decoration. There were three to choose from, and I chose the middle tunnel, figuring that it was more likely to head downwards, rather than circle around the castle.

I followed it, relieved when it started to descend in a steep trajectory. It was dimly lit, but there was more than enough light for me to find my way. Before long, I came to a door, its frame sunk back into the stone wall.

Expecting the door to be locked, I was surprised when it creaked open, cobwebs dropping from the ceiling as it did so. Clearly this door hadn't been opened in a while...It wouldn't be what I was looking for. Still, I decided to explore the room anyway and see if it led elsewhere.

It was mostly empty, apart from a few overturned barrels that someone had used as tables, old candles glued to their surfaces with overflowing wax. As I walked further in, my eyes were drawn to the floor. Marked on the stone surface was a huge rune—the exact same one Ruby and I had seen in the village. Thankfully, this version wasn't created in blood, but a black charcoal or paint.

I don't understand.

Why was the same rune here? I'd originally thought that it had something to do with an uprising against the Hellswans, but now I wasn't so sure. If Queen Trina's palace was the hotbed for an anti-Tejus revolution, I thought I would have noticed...or been invited along.

I looked around, trying to see if there were any further clues as to the meaning of the rune. At the far end of the room, behind the door, was a small iron square about two foot in length and height, with an iron ring at its center. Out of curiosity more than anything else, I pulled at it—and the iron square came away from the wall. It was unexpectedly heavy, and I dropped it, causing a clatter that reverberated around the room.

Crap.

A hole had been revealed in the wall, looking out onto pitch black.

"Hello!" A voice came from within…a female voice.

"Ruby?"

"Ash!" she cried back. I leaned against the wall for a second, the energy knocked out of me as relief seeped into my bones.

"Ash?" she called again. "Is that you?"

"It's me—I'm coming," I replied hastily.

This obviously wasn't the main entrance, but it was better than nothing. I could just about squeeze through the hole—the only problem was not knowing if there was going to be a fifty-foot drop beneath me or just solid ground, and it was too dark at the point of this entrance to use True Sight. I shuffled forward on my stomach, feeling my way with my hands. Once my torso was fully through the hole, I grappled mid-air, trying to feel for a landing.

My hands touched cold stone, and I pulled my body forward.

"I'm in," I called to Ruby.

As my eyes adjusted to the dark, I could just make out a narrow path in front of me, and the outline of doors on the left-hand side—all chained shut.

"I'm so glad you're here!" she whispered. I could sense the same relief in her that I'd experienced a few moments ago. It wouldn't be long now.

"I don't think I'm alone though…when I was shouting for you I think I heard another voice…" Ruby trailed off. I listened, alert and tense – hoping that it wasn't one of Queen Trina's guards.

"Help…please." I jumped as the voice called softly out of the darkness, coming from the cell closest to me.

"Ruby…Ash…please, I'm here," it continued, the voice so frail I could only just hear it.

"Julian!" Ruby responded. "Julian—is that you?"

"It's me."

I looked into the nearest cell. This one was different from the others—there were no bars on the door, just a thick black block with a small hole in it. I looked through, but could only see a hump of shadow in the far corner.

"Julian?" I spoke though the hole. "Are you all right?"

The hump moved, and shakily dragged itself to its feet. Painfully slowly, the shape moved toward the door. Now I could get a better look at his face, and what I saw chilled me to the bone. He was gaunt to the point of emaciation, and his eyes bulged with untold horrors.

"Hi, Ash," he whispered. "I'm so glad you're here."

"Me too." I gulped. Here just in time—it didn't look like Julian would have been able to hold on for much longer. I felt sick. Sick at what Queen Trina had been doing to him while the entire time I'd been above, eating like a king and living in the lap of luxury.

"Can you get me out?" he asked quietly, and I didn't hear a shred of hope in his voice.

"I will," I replied. "I need to check on Ruby, and then I'll be right back, okay?"

"Okay," he agreed.

I turned away from him, hating myself for feeling relieved that I could do so—the despair and dejection in his eyes was tough to take. I wondered if Julian would ever make a full recovery from this.

I walked down to the rest of the cells, checking each one to see if Ruby was inside. I found her at the far end, near a door that looked like it was the main entrance to the dungeon.

"Hey," I exhaled on seeing her. Her hands were wrapped around the bars, and I closed mine over them, noticing how cold they were.

"Thanks for showing up." She smiled up at me.

"You trying to make a habit of getting locked up, shortie?" I asked, trying to pretend that I was fine—that I didn't utterly despise myself for letting this happen.

She smiled bleakly, then replied in a quiet voice, "Is Julian okay? He didn't sound so good."

"He'll be fine when he gets out of here," I lied.

She nodded, her eyes downcast.

"He would have been down here for so long."

I didn't want her to dwell on it, so I smiled reassuringly and stood back from the door.

"I need to find something to get you out of here." I eyed the narrow passage, hoping I would find something suitably sharp to cut through the chains. Using True Sight, I looked in the direction of Julian's cell. Behind the furthest wall there was an old armory—full to the brim with axes and swords that didn't look like they'd been used in the last hundred years.

"I'll be back," I promised her.

"Hurry," she whispered. "I'm worried Queen Trina's going to recover."

I hastened back toward Julian's cell, hoping I could find a door that would lead through to the armory. There was nothing but solid stone wall. I kicked it in frustration, sending dust and debris clattering down from the ceiling. Realizing that the wall was about as old as the equipment in the armory, I started to kick the different stones in the wall. If just one would give, then I could reach through and remove a weapon.

I tried a few, but they wouldn't budge, but then with the fifth kick, one of the larger stones moved. I pushed it with my hands, gently easing it out of the crumbling cement. Finally, it gave way and, with a satisfying thump, landed backward in the armory. I heard the clatter of swords and other weapons that had been lined up against the wall—and hoped that we were far enough away from anyone for it not to have been heard.

"Ash, are you okay?" Ruby hissed.

"I'm fine," I replied, then fell silent, waiting to hear if anyone was heading our way. When nothing happened I reached in and felt around with my hand until it lighted on a particularly fierce-looking axe.

Perfect.

I withdrew it from the armory.

It was dull and old, but it was still sharp.

"I'm going to try Julian first," I called to Ruby.

"Okay!"

I peered through the hole in Julian's cell door.

"Stand back, Julian," I instructed him, and he shuffled back toward the end of the cell. Putting all my strength behind it, I slammed the axe down on the lock. The impact shook the handle of the axe, and my arms trembled along with it. The lock clattered loudly, and part of it dropped to the floor. The door swung open.

I opened it, waiting for Julian to come out. He glanced between the open door and me, his eyes wary and watchful. I stood back, trying to give him some space—maybe he just needed to do it in his own time.

"I'm going to get Ruby out," I told him, walking away from the cell door.

I repeated the action at Ruby's cell door, but as soon as it swung open, she shot out, throwing herself into my arms.

I closed my eyes, inhaling the smell of her hair. I felt like I'd almost lost her—the night of the trial, when Tejus had told me that Ruby had been with Commander Varga, I'd thought the worst.

"You scared me," I murmured into her hair.

"You should have listened to me," she gently reprimanded me.

"I know, I know—and believe me, there's nothing I've ever regretted more. I'm so sorry, Ruby. Forgive me? I was arrogant and stupid."

She punched me. "Yeah, you were… But you saved my ass *again*, so you're forgiven."

I held her tightly for a few moments, and then she untangled herself.

"I need to see Julian." She looked past my arm to where he stood—silently, at the opposite end of the dungeon. She approached him slowly, as if he was a wild animal. By the look of him, the assumption wasn't that far off.

"Julian?" she asked softly.

"Ruby," he replied. "I didn't think you would ever find me."

"It's okay now, we're here—we're going to get back home. It's going to be okay." She spoke to him in a soothing, soft voice and I could see his body starting to tremble. I couldn't imagine what the poor boy had been through—thinking he was all alone here, probably imagining that his friends had already gone home…and left him? I didn't know so much about their relationships with one another, but they had always struck me as a tight-knit group—though all alone in a dark, dank cellar, I could imagine that it wouldn't take long for people to doubt that they were ever going to be rescued.

"We need to get out of here," I announced, starting to worry that I'd been gone too long already. If Queen Trina found me missing when she recovered, she would know something was up. I could only hope that her wounds were severe enough to keep her down for a while.

I looked around with True Sight, working out the best way to get out. I decided on the main entrance that I hadn't used yet. It appeared to lead out onto another long hallway, and then gardens beyond that.

"This way," I commanded, leading them toward the door.

"I don't think Julian can go very fast," Ruby warned.

"I'm fine," he argued. "Let's just get out of here. *Please*."

I opened the door and we walked swiftly along the hallway. Julian was lagging, but Ruby helped him along while I kept my eyes and ears out for ministers or guards coming this way. I prayed that the usually deserted palace would stay that way.

Once we were in the gardens, I looked around for the stables. We were at the opposite end of the palace to where I'd been staying, and so to get to the road out of the kingdom would take longer here. On foot we also had a larger chance of being stopped and questioned by guards. If we didn't have bull-horses, we wouldn't make it out in time.

Looking around once more, I finally found them.

"We need to get to the stables." I motioned in the direction we should head. "Stick to the trees and walls—try to avoid walking out in plain sight, okay?"

Ruby and Julian nodded.

As swiftly as we could, we navigated the small path that led away from the palace. Thankfully it was surrounded by yellow-fruit trees, and their leaves provided us some camouflage. I didn't even know for certain that anyone was watching, but I knew better than to leave it to chance. I had a suspicion that nothing went unnoticed by Queen Trina in her kingdom.

We made it to the stables. I exhaled some of the tension that had been building up in me since finding Ruby, and went to fetch us some bull-horses.

I ran straight into a guard.

"Ashbik." He nodded in greeting. "How is the queen?"

"She's recovering well," I bluffed.

"Those trials." He shook his head. "Too dangerous."

"I completely agree. Which is, incidentally, why I'm here—I'm going to speak with the Impartial Ministers. See if these trials can't be cut short."

"Good. Do you need transport?"

"For two," I replied as firmly as I could. "I am going to ask one of the Impartial Ministers to return with me—confront him with Queen Trina's wounds."

The guard nodded enthusiastically.

"I like your thinking! Let me know if there's anything I can do to help."

"Just the bull-horses," I replied.

Soon I was walking two creatures out of the stables while the guard saluted me, pride in his eyes.

I waited till I was out of view, then had to circle back around to where Ruby and Julian were hiding by the trees.

"Was everything okay?" Ruby asked with a worried frown.

"Fine. We just need to be quick."

I put Ruby on her own bull-horse, while Julian rode with me. He was so frail that the creature didn't appear to notice there was a human on its back. As a result, it balked and whinnied until I jumped on, just at the moment that Julian looked like he was going to go flying off.

"Whoa there!" I calmed the creature, and then, with Ruby riding by my side, we headed off at a brisk trot in the direction of the main entrance.

"STOP!"

I glanced over my shoulder to see the guard who'd just provided me with the bull-horses. His face was now contorted with rage as he identified Ruby, and no doubt Julian as the human he'd probably had a hand in locking in the dungeon.

"*Ride!*" I called out to Ruby, and we both started to gallop.

Up ahead I could see more guards circling around the courtyard. Both groups would eventually meet in the middle, blocking the entrance.

Thinking quickly, I grabbed Ruby's hand, leaning toward her as the bull-horse galloped at full speed. Not wanting to, but knowing that I didn't have a choice, I syphoned off her swiftly. As the horses reached the courtyard entrance, I created a barrier on either side of us—just wide enough to allow the horses to pass through.

The guards hollered angrily, but we didn't let up on our pace.

Soon the hooves of the bull-horses were kicking up dust on the open road back to Hellswan. Ruby was safe, and she was with me. I glanced over at her and she grinned.

I love you, shortie, I said to myself. *And one day the whole world's going to know it.*

HAZEL

I had tried to dissuade Tejus from coming with me to revisit the Viking graveyard, but he wouldn't hear of it—and secretly I was glad that I wouldn't have to face my brother alone. Rationally, I knew that Benedict couldn't help what was happening to him and that during the day it was likely that Benedict would once again return to normal...but I couldn't help the faint sense of unease that had been with me all morning, and the reluctance to face Benedict after last night—not one hundred percent sure about what I'd find.

It made me feel like a horrific sister, and deeply ashamed.

We had also brought along a group of five ministers. I hoped that they would be able to somehow unlock the door of the temple, but I wasn't holding out much hope. The ministers' ability to do anything other than whisper didn't exactly fill me with confidence. Still, it was currently the only help we had available to us and I was willing to try anything.

We were flying to the graveyard with the vultures. I had chosen to sit behind Tejus, careful to avoid his chest wounds. They were healing at a rapid pace, but from the occasional wince, and his still-dull pallor, I could tell that Tejus hadn't fully recovered. In the first few moments of the flight, I'd tried to cling on by tightening my thighs on the bird's body. Tejus had turned around with a scowl on his face, and then proceeded to take my hands and wrap them around his waist, holding them there tightly with one hand.

There was so much I wanted to say to Tejus. I hadn't forgotten the promise I'd made to myself last night; I wanted to tell him how I felt, and that I knew that whatever was holding him back, we could overcome it, move past it, whatever. And if he wasn't convinced? Then at least I'd told him—I'd given it one last shot. Without that, I didn't think I'd ever be able to move on or get over him. I figured Nevertide would haunt me enough without that hanging over me too.

I rested my head against his back. Now wasn't the time to talk—it would have to be after we spoke with my brother. I was content just to be in this moment: my body pressed against his, neither of us in any immediate danger and miles above both Hellswan castle and our destination—free, just for the moment.

All too soon, the group of us landed in the graveyard. We made our way over to the temple, finding it locked with the hole still covered. I looked at Tejus.

"Is he in there?" I asked.

"Yes."

"Do you know if he's…"

"He seems like he's himself," Tejus replied, answering my unspoken question.

"Okay." I nodded, mentally preparing myself. "I need to get to the door."

We walked over to the natural land dip where the door to the entrance lay, and I leaned against it once again.

"Benedict? It's Hazel," I called out.

"Hazel?" His voice came from behind the door. It was weak and sounded confused. If the entity was gaining power, then it stood to reason that Benedict was finding it harder to shake the creature off. I'd have gone half-mad anyway, spending my days locked up in a creepy temple, with or without an entity habitually invading my mind.

"I'm so sorry, Benedict," I called to him.

"I-It's okay. I don't think I was at the castle last night anyway…I didn't come back with a stone. Was I there?"

I looked at Tejus, who returned my gaze with a calm expression. It was up to me.

"No," I replied, "you weren't there."

"Good." He sighed.

"Benedict," I continued, "I've got some ministers here, and they're going to have a look and see if they can open the door—is that okay?"

"They won't be able to. No one can get in or out. That's the way he wants it."

"I know—but we need to try," I pressed.

I could practically hear his unenthusiastic shrug. Had it not felt so heart-breaking, it would have been comforting that I could still predict my brother's mannerisms…when he was himself.

"Okay," he said.

"I'll come back and talk to you in a bit."

I stood aside, and the ministers gathered around the door. I walked back up the slope and joined Tejus as he watched them work.

"What do you think about the stones?" I asked. "Why didn't he return with any of them?"

Tejus shook his head grimly.

"I don't know…it doesn't really make much sense. I thought that perhaps there were stones kept in our living quarters, but why not just blow the door in? It should have been easy for him—it's exactly what he did at Danto's tower."

Our living quarters?

I felt an intense heat creep up my neck, and tried to ignore what he'd just said. Obviously it was just a slip of the tongue, and besides, we had far more pressing matters on our hands…*but.*

"What?" Tejus asked, looking at me in confusion.

"Nothing," I replied too quickly.

He gave me a peculiar look, and I turned my attention to the ministers who were muttering and gesticulating around the door of the temple. It looked like they were performing some kind of ritual.

"I was thinking the same thing," I replied eventually. "About why Benedict couldn't get into my room. The frustration in his voice…all the pleading. It seemed like a lot of effort just to scare me or make me upset. There must have been some reason that he wanted to get in there."

"And why he couldn't," Tejus agreed.

I thought about last night. If the entity was using Benedict to try to manipulate me, rather than just use brute force, then it meant he still didn't have much power…but why not? He had full control of Benedict, and had syphoned the energy off at least half the castle so far.

"Okay, we know that the stones are the key to unlocking him and giving him power," I started, thinking out loud, "and so he needs those…but in that case, why did he even bother going to Danto's tower in the first place? Why not just get Benedict to take all the stones from the passageway— that's easiest for him, right? Why even go into the castle at all?"

"It's a pattern," Tejus murmured. "He must need only certain stones—or stones removed in a particular order…and if so, then somewhere in my tower, there's another lock…" He trailed off.

"The stone is what gave him the power last time," I added. "In Danto's tower—the reason he could syphon off you so aggressively and knock us back. He must then lose power when he can't get to a specific stone—which is why he couldn't get into the room without my help."

Tejus nodded.

"We need to find the next lock, and guard it. We could end all this before he rises to full power."

I was silent. I wasn't sure it was going to be that simple. I felt there were still so many things we didn't understand, like the role the Acolytes were playing in all this, why they had murdered Varga, and just how much Queen Trina knew about Benedict and the stones—and the entity.

The ministers came over before I could question Tejus any further.

"Your highness," one of them muttered, "there is nothing we can do—it's not a barrier that we understand. It is a powerful force that we can't penetrate or disable. We wouldn't even know where to begin."

A huge surprise, I thought uncharitably.

"Keep trying—anything that you think might help," Tejus commanded. "Consult the Impartial Ministers, do whatever it takes, but I want that door opened."

The minister bowed his head in acknowledgment, and returned to the door.

Once he was gone, Tejus cleared his throat. "I need to return to the Fells. There's a meeting to discuss the last trial. I need to be there," he informed me.

"Are you up for that?" I asked, privately thinking that he still didn't look completely healed and would have been better off staying indoors—and far, far away from the Impartial Ministers and the trials.

"Yes."

The reply was curt, and I smiled to myself. I didn't think

that Tejus would ever admit to being in any kind of pain, physical or otherwise. It made him *impossible,* but I knew a lot of men back in The Shade like that—my dad, grandfather and uncle included.

"I'm going to stay here with the ministers and keep Benedict company," I replied, knowing that I wouldn't be able to talk him out of attending the meeting.

"I'd rather you didn't. It's not safe, and there's nothing more you can do for your brother right now."

"I disagree—I can keep him company. That's what he needs right now. He's all alone, Tejus. I can't just leave him here," I argued.

"And I can't focus if I think you're in danger," he retorted.

I sighed.

"Tejus, I'm always in danger. Here or at the castle—it never stops coming. Haven't you noticed that already?"

"I am all too aware of that, but here you're right where the entity is going to be—and presumably the Acolytes use this place too. The ministers are next to useless; at least I know that the entity can't reach you in my chambers."

"This isn't up for discussion, Tejus—I'm sorry. I'm staying with my brother."

He scowled at me, clearly furious but for once trying to hold his tongue.

"I'll leave before nightfall," I promised him.

Tejus growled and then cursed under his breath. I appreciated how difficult this was for him—I knew that he needed to feel like he was protecting me at all times, and would have felt that he had failed dismally at that lately, but I also knew that my brother needed me.

"You'd better," he warned.

Or what? I thought facetiously.

"I will," I replied instead, not wanting to enrage him further.

"Lithan, Qentos!" he barked at the group of ministers, "We're leaving. Praxus, make sure Hazel is home before nightfall. Hours before."

He stalked off, Lithan and Qentos stumbling over the uneven surfaces of the cove in their effort to keep up. I watched Tejus depart, and then weaved my way through the group of ministers around the door.

I wanted to speak to my brother in the short time we had left.

TEJUS

The meeting was over.

All had long since departed, and I had dismissed Lithan and Qentos. I was left alone in the empty pavilion, the sunset staining the ivory white of its structure a deep red. I should have left hours ago, but I had a decision to make—one that left me feeling completely adrift from the carefully orchestrated plans I had envisioned for myself.

There were three more trials left before the emperor would be announced.

For the first time since they had begun, I was seriously questioning my ability to succeed.

When the ghoul had taken a swipe at me, the feeling had

been utterly soul-destroying. Not the pain of the wound, that was a mere scratch. It was as if the repugnant creature had left something inside of me—or taken something out. My insides felt utterly empty, as if its touch had sucked the life from me. My entire body hurt, and was plagued by an exhaustion that I couldn't shake. Syphoning off Hazel had helped, but only temporarily.

The Impartial Ministers, in their smug, self-satisfied way, had apologized for the trial and their part in it, but they would not slow down the process. It would all begin again tomorrow, and I could not fight—I had little mental energy left. Just controlling the vulture to the graveyard and then using True Sight to see Hazel's brother had wiped me out. The ride here had been even harder.

I didn't understand it.

The night of the ghouls, I could have sworn on my life that I'd seen Queen Trina Seraq attacked in much the same way, but nothing seemed to have been troubling her in the same way during the meeting—if anything, she seemed livelier than I had ever witnessed before. Perhaps I was wrong, and she hadn't been injured—it had just been wishful thinking on my part.

I thought about what my mother had said in the dream, and the way the entity had addressed me.

False king.

It was a label I did not like. Was this some higher power proving my inadequacy against those who were better suited to rule? Memenion and Hadalix were the only kings left. Memenion would do a good job—he was a righteous and honorable man, but I knew he didn't want the position as some might. His kingdom had always remained so isolated and removed from the politics of Nevertide, would he truly have the ability to rule all the kingdoms? Hadalix I believed to be inadequate for the position—he lacked the courage and the foresight...which would then leave Queen Trina. A vicious and ruthless ruler, who would not be around long enough to enjoy the spoils of emperorship if I discovered that she was involved in Varga's death.

I had felt that the crown was mine for the taking.

Yet my own dead mother had disagreed with me. What had she said? That there was a different path open to me...that I could follow my true destiny.

I had a difficult time envisioning what that could possibly be. Though even Hazel had told me that I had a choice—that I could forge a different path for myself than the one I had already mapped out. Yet I had no idea if I even wanted to. I had no idea what such a thing might even look like...

Don't you?

Hazel's face, calm and clear, appeared in my consciousness.

But she was out of my reach. She would never wish to stay here, to rule by my side as queen in a land that she detested, far removed from her family and friends—and I would never allow her to make that choice to become a sentry. Not when there was a chance that she would regret it forever, and come to loathe me. I could not stand it.

With a sigh, I walked away from the pavilion. Pausing by the arch where my friend had breathed his last, I placed my hand on the cold stone in memory. What I wouldn't give for his advice now—now, when no road looked clear to me, and I had impossible choices to make.

Hazel

He hadn't returned.

I paced up and down the living room, watching the sun sinking deeper and wondering where on earth he could be. I'd seen both Lithan and Qentos arrive by bird, but no Tejus. I'd gone down to find them, to ask where he was, but they had vanished completely, and so I'd ended up returning to my room, frustrated and worried. I had seen a few ministers in the hallways, but none of them knew where their king was, and dismissed me quickly—hurrying off in the opposite direction.

I leaned against the window, trying to spot his bird approaching from the direction of the Fells. Eventually I saw something flying toward the castle, and hastily wiped away the condensation that I'd caused on the window. It was a vulture. And as it became larger, I could recognize the posture of Tejus, and sighed with relief. He was home.

Wanting to meet him in the courtyard, I turned to leave the tower.

I raced down the staircase and along the main corridor.

"Hazel!"

An achingly familiar voice stopped me in my tracks.

Ruby?

I spun around, and saw the familiar blonde hair and blue eyes of my friend. I started to run toward her, disbelieving and overjoyed at the same time. She hugged me, and I felt a lump form in the back of my throat.

"I missed you," I whispered hoarsely.

"Me too," she replied. I waved at Ash, who was standing behind her. He smiled back in greeting, but took a step back, giving us some space.

"We've got some good news!" Ruby exclaimed. "It's a long story, but Julian's safe! He's in the human quarters right now recovering."

I stared at Ruby in astonishment, and then I exhaled. I felt as if I'd been carrying around a huge hiker's backpack without realizing it, and suddenly someone had come along and removed about half of its contents. Only then was I aware just how heavy that load had been, and just how freeing it was to have it removed.

"Oh, thank God," I whispered.

Ruby nodded. She knew how I felt—I could see the same relief in her eyes.

"We dropped him off in the human quarters and then came to find you. Is everything okay? You looked like you were in a hurry."

"It's far from okay, but let's go and see him now." I grimaced.

I glanced briefly behind me, hoping I would catch sight of Tejus entering the castle. He wasn't anywhere to be seen, but I would find him later.

Julian was in his and Benedict's room, sitting up in bed with Jenney by his side. Yelena was sitting on Benedict's bed, hugging one of his pillows to her chest.

"Hey." I smiled at Julian.

He returned the smile, and my heart constricted. He looked *so* ill. He was severely malnourished and the bones of his face jutted out painfully.

"Both Julian and I managed to get locked up in Queen Trina's dungeon," Ruby stated. "It wasn't a great place to be."

I nodded, taking a moment to let the rage that was free-flowing through my veins subside. I took a few deep breaths, not wanting Julian to have to hear my ranting when he was obviously so unwell.

"How are you feeling?" I asked him.

"Better now that I'm here. I had thought you'd all be home by now."

"We wouldn't have left without you!" I replied.

"That's what I keep telling him," Ruby added.

She mock-glared at Julian, and he rolled his eyes. It was the only indication he'd given so far that it was still Julian in there and not just a broken husk of a kid who had been through far too much.

"Do you want to rest?" Jenney asked Julian solicitously.

He nodded weakly, then coughed with bone-shaking intensity. I smiled, not wanting Julian to know how alarmed I was by his health. I was glad that Jenney seemed to be taking up the role of nurse—I hoped that she would have some medicine to give him, or know someone who would.

Ash, Ruby, Yelena and I all traipsed out of the room. Under instruction from Jenney, Yelena went off to fetch extra blankets from the servant quarters. When we were alone, I turned to Ruby.

"I'm glad you found him when you did." I swallowed. It

didn't look like Julian would have survived Queen Trina's dungeons for much longer. Ruby nodded, wrapping her arms around her body to comfort herself.

"We're going to kill her, right?" I added, looking at Ash.

He looked faintly surprised at my statement—I was only half joking.

"Something needs to be done," he replied. "Though from what I've heard, Tejus has it in for the queen after Varga's death."

"What?" Ruby burst out.

Ash belatedly realized that Ruby hadn't known about the commander.

"I'm so sorry," he replied. "He was killed."

Ruby went completely white.

"Sit down," I told her, walking her over to one of the sofas.

"I don't understand!" she exploded. "He was going back to Hellswan castle—I thought he was safe…"

I looked at Ash, who shook his head, his eyes pleading.

"I'm so sorry. He was one of the few good sentries here," I said, putting my arms around my shocked friend.

I then proceeded to tell her the series of events that had taken place in her absence: the runes found by Varga's body, Benedict becoming possessed by the entity, what had happened to Yelena and Benedict's mention of Queen Trina's involvement—and how I truly believed she was part of the Acolyte cult somehow. When I was finished, Ruby's eyes were wide as saucers, and she had remained as white as a ghost.

"I had something to tell you—about the rune. I saw one when I was staying in Memenion's castle. It's tied to an old cult, originating from his kingdom…but I guess you knew that already?"

"Not that Memenion's kingdom had anything to do with it." I frowned. "Maybe Tejus and I have been looking at the wrong history books…"

"They're all really friendly there. I'm sure they wouldn't mind helping us."

"What were you doing there anyway?" I asked.

"I was on my way here when the ice fires began. Commander Varga stopped me at the Hellswan border and took me to Memenion's kingdom. Then he was supposed to ride back here. And I got thrown in Trina's dungeons before Ash came to the rescue—again." She smiled up at him, and I resisted the urge to snigger. I'd never really seen Ruby behave that way before toward a boy. She was normally so tough and resilient; to see her make moon eyes kind of turned the Ruby I knew on her head.

"Where did you hear that Tejus had it in for Queen Trina?" I asked Ash, trying to make sense of events—as far as I was aware, the only person Tejus had mentioned that to was me.

"He threatened her in full view of everyone," he replied, "at the Fells. So she knows he's on to her—but I imagine that she thinks she's untouchable, or that there won't be any evidence to connect her to his murder."

I nodded. "It was a bold move to jail Ruby after that. Maybe she *does* think she's untouchable. If she does it will work in our favor. She'll make riskier moves, and then it won't just be us who believe she's dangerous."

Tejus hadn't told me that he'd threatened Queen Trina. Privately I wanted to cheer—I was so glad that he'd finally said something to her...and it eradicated any fears I might have had, no matter how small, that he still had feelings for her.

"So is Benedict in the temple now?" Ruby asked.

"He will be until nightfall, then he'll come here again, I think. Tejus and I have a theory about the stones—that the entity needs to remove them in a specific pattern in order to regain his full strength." I had spent some time in his quarters looking for a stone lock, but hadn't found anything. I didn't think that meant our theory was wrong—I just hadn't found the location yet, and would probably need Tejus's help to do so.

"Do you think when the entity has enough power, he'll release Benedict?" Ruby asked me quietly.

"I have to believe that."

It was the one thing that kept me hanging on at the moment—that and knowing I wasn't in any of this alone. We were all going through our own private hells. Knowing Ruby and Julian had survived theirs left me feeling hopeful that Benedict would also overcome the entity's hold over him.

"So what's next?" Ruby asked. "What do we do now—do we wait for Benedict to return tonight and try to keep him here?"

"Exactly," I replied. "But it's easier said than done; he's managed to syphon nearly every minister and guard in this castle, leaving them completely wiped out. He's untouchable."

"We'll find a way," Ruby reassured me. "There's always a way."

"You need to rest first," Ash commented, looking pointedly at Ruby.

"We have a couple of hours before he's due—it's normally late in the night. Probably just to freak us out more," I muttered.

"What are you going to do?" Ruby asked.

"See Tejus…he's not well at the moment. The last trial, when Queen Trina lost her powers, he was attacked by one of the ghouls, and I don't think he's made a full recovery yet."

"The next trial's tomorrow," Ash replied, frowning. "Why hasn't he recovered?"

I shrugged. "I don't actually know. I guess the combination of being syphoned by the entity and then the ministers, and *then* being attacked by the ghoul, was too much."

Ash looked puzzled, but didn't say anything.

"What?" I pressed. If he had information about Tejus then I wanted to know.

"Nothing. Nothing really…it's just that sentries have pretty good healing powers. But perhaps you're right—that's a lot. I'm sure he'll be fine."

"Of course he'll be fine!" I answered hotly.

"He will be," Ash repeated. I wasn't entirely sure if he meant it or he was trying to pacify me. I chose to ignore him either way—the idea that Tejus wouldn't heal was unthinkable. And anyway, today he'd been up and flown to the Fells without a problem. He'd just looked a bit pale, that was all.

"I need to fill him in on all this, he'll want to know about Queen Trina," I announced, rising up from the sofa.

Ruby smiled. "Tell him we said hi."

"Well, hang on," Ash added, looking mildly flustered. "I'm not entirely sure I'm welcome here…the ministers here are going to see me as a traitor. At a time like this, I doubt they're going to feel very happy about me staying in the castle. Perhaps *you* could ask Tejus? Say that I'm not willing to leave Ruby?"

"It will be fine." I smirked. "Once he hears what happened to Ruby and Julian he'll just be happy that you saved them. I promise."

"Will he?" Ruby exclaimed.

"Yeah." I smiled weakly. "He's… changed."

A look of understanding passed across Ruby's face, and she eyed me knowingly. "Right." She smiled.

"It's not like that…not for *him,* anyway."

"Hang on." Ruby laughed. "Tejus of Hellswan suddenly cares about your friends to the extent of putting his most valued guards on a manhunt for Julian, does everything he can to save your brother, and then won't mind that his trial opponent and an ex-council member of Queen Trina's stays in his castle… and you don't think he feels anything for you?

Are you *mad?*"

She didn't understand. And I wasn't about to go into detail about the conversations Tejus and I had had about the potential of us having a relationship. He might have cared, but not enough to put aside whatever was bothering and holding him back from me...not yet, anyway.

Ash stared at the ceiling. Clearly this conversation was uncomfortable for him.

"I'm leaving now," I said to Ruby. "Before Ash has a fit."

I knew Ash's views of the Hellswans. It didn't bother me in the slightest—he too would see that Tejus had changed. And I had faith that Tejus would turn Nevertide around. He just had to find his own way of doing it.

"I'll come and find you later," Ruby said.

"Okay."

I said goodbye to Ash and then hurried out of the room. I was desperate to see Tejus—maybe together we could work out a way to speed up his recovery. I would need him tonight.

I entered his living room, calling his name. Only Lucifer appeared when I called, and apart from the moody lynx, Tejus's chambers were completely empty.

Where is he?

TEJUS

The room was full. Most were seated, but some had needed to stand—mainly the guard superiors, though Varga's lieutenant had taken up my friend's empty chair. While I'd waited for them to all file in, I'd been transfixed by my father's portrait on the wall. I had seen that painting thousands of times, but tonight the sense of foreboding that usually accompanied it was absent. I realized that I pitied him. He had lacked foresight and the ability to relinquish control, that much was evident from his actions in removing the stone from the entity lock. He must have been desperate for Jenus to rule—the one sentry in all of Nevertide, with the possible exception of Queen Trina, who was wholly unworthy of the title of emperor.

I felt sick at the reality of what I was about to do. But it would give me one thing—the chance to fix the mistakes my father had made. Hopefully, that would sever any last ties I had to the man. No matter how hard I tried for it to be otherwise, he was a dark shadow looming over me, and I wanted to be rid of him once and for all.

"Before you begin, King Tejus, pray tell us what Memenion is doing here?' Lithan asked angrily, glaring at the king, who in turn was too perplexed by my request himself to look affronted.

"Don't question me, Lithan," I snapped. I wasn't entirely sure why I'd asked the king along either. I supposed I just wanted him to hear the news from me—and if I was completely honest with myself, he was now one of the only people I trusted, and, in a way, a link to Varga. My friend had thought well of him, and so now would I.

"I apologize for the late hour, but thank you all for coming." I hesitated.

Are you really going to do this?

I swallowed, trying to find the courage to continue.

"I am afraid I will no longer take part in the imperial trials. I also need to relinquish my position as Hellswan king. I rose to power through the trials with an advantage that would not have been permitted had any of you known about it—I had in my possession one of the entity stones. It gave me an advantage, one that I am not convinced that I would have succeeded without."

I had said my piece. There was deathly silence for a few, long, moments—and then the room broke simultaneously into raucous complaint.

"This is insanity!" Lithan cried. "Why are you doing this?"

"How could you have defiled your family name in such a way?" the minister of ceremonies demanded. "It is pure scandal!"

"Your Highness—Your highness! Tell us all this is some gross misunderstanding. You are our rightful king, no other, Tejus!" Qentos quivered. "It is Varga's death! It has affected your mind—you need to *rest,* your highness!"

Other shouts exploded forth in the same vein, and I waited for the commotion to die down before I spoke again. I wasn't sure how I felt. My gaze met the eyes of King Memenion. He was the only one not protesting. Instead he wore a speculative expression, and I imagined he was trying to understand my motives. I wasn't sure even I understood what they fully were—there was the injury of course, but I struggled trying to convince myself that it was that factor alone.

"I understand that you are all confused. And I will try to answer your questions as best I can." They all clamored to be answered at once, and I raised my hand to silence them before continuing. "However, there is a more pressing matter. The trials will continue tomorrow, and we need to find a replacement for the Hellswan champion. I suggest Ashbik, whom I believe might well have bested me were it not for the stone. I ask you to consider him as my replacement."

"Madness! Sheer madness!" Lithan cried.

"Why?" I asked him. "He is an adequate replacement."

Lithan spluttered some more before he could respond.

"Well, for one, he is currently the advisor to Queen Trina—he is a betrayer!"

"No, he's not!" A voice sounded out from the far end of the room. I sighed. I *really* should have asked one of the guards to keep an eye on her.

"He's here!" Hazel exclaimed, scrambling out from the minister's office that she'd been hiding in at the last council meeting. I had been so preoccupied with what I was about to tell the ministers that I'd completely failed to detect her.

"GET OUT!" Lithan screeched at her.

"Lithan! Silence!" I ordered. "Let her speak."

"He's here—in the castle," Hazel repeated. "He no longer

works for Queen Trina. She put Ruby and Julian in the dungeon, and Ash rescued them. If he goes back there, he's dead."

"That is inconsequential!" Lithan exploded. "The fact remains that Ashbik is still a traitor and doesn't belong in the kitchens of Hellswan—let alone at the head of it!"

I was doing my utmost to hide my fury. Queen Trina *again*. Did the woman have a death wish? I vowed this would be the last time that she harmed any soul from my kingdom—human or sentry.

My eyes met Hazel's briefly, then I had to look away. I couldn't read what was going through her mind. She had obviously heard my speech, and I couldn't tell if she pitied me or if it was something else, but when she'd looked at me her eyes had been soft—loving? That didn't make sense to me. Not after what I'd just done. If I wasn't emperor, then I had no hope of saving her brother. I had expected her to be furious.

"You need to leave, Hazel," I told her calmly. "This is a council meeting. Go to the human quarters—I will come and find you later."

I had expected her to argue, but she agreed meekly and abruptly left the room. I watched her go, wondering what she would have to say to me later.

I cleared my throat. "I would like you to reconsider your opinion. Lithan, try not to let your prejudice stand in the way. He is a good contender. His brief alignment with Queen Trina may well give him an edge."

Lithan glanced over at Memenion.

"Do not concern yourself with me," the king replied to Lithan. "I believe that the right sentry will win the trials. As long as that isn't Queen Trina Seraq, then I am satisfied. I too believe that Ashbik is a good contender."

I sighed with relief. Memenion's opinion would hold sway with some of the more open-minded ministers.

"Please, Tejus—what is the meaning of this?" Qentos quivered again. All the ministers and guards went completely silent.

Now what?

"The attack by the ghoul weakened me. The chances of me succeeding at the next trial are slim—too slim to risk this kingdom losing its seat of power. There is a malevolent being here that above all has to be contained. We are all in mortal danger if this creature rises. If Queen Trina takes the kingdom, then I fear for us all. We cannot allow this to happen. I am hoping that Memenion and Ashbik will work together to ensure she is not victorious—and I believe they will." Memenion nodded in my direction, and I acknowledged his approval. "And because this is the right thing to do—the honorable thing to do. I am not my father; I will not follow in his footsteps. The people of this kingdom cheered for Ashbik because they believed that he would create radical change. I want to give him the opportunity to do so. My people need him more than they need me."

And because I am in love. I am completely, impossibly in love with a human. She has torn away the very foundations of my belief, and I no longer wish to be the man I was. I want her to be mine, without having to change who she is—because she is my better. My superior in every single way imaginable.

The truth I had been searching for hit me with sudden, irrevocable clarity.

"I have to go," I stated.

"What?" Lithan screamed. "We have not decided! We must settle this matter at once—and if your mind can't be swayed from this ridiculousness, then we need to discuss a more adequate replacement!"

I smiled at Lithan.

"It is Ashbik you need, Lithan. If you're worried about your position, I can put in a good word for you. Despite your ruthlessness, you do have some more redeeming qualities that Ashbik may approve of," I commented dryly, "such as your lowly birth. That might endear you to him."

Lithan stuttered, sounding like he was being strangled, his face turning an unattractive shade of mottled red.

"Lieutenant, take over; fight for Ashbik. Trust me on this if nothing else."

I turned and headed to the door. I hadn't even left the room when I heard Lithan suggesting that Jenus be brought back from his banishment. Thankfully, Memenion's laughter at his suggestion could be heard all the way out in the hallway.

The ministers would come around eventually. They didn't really have any other choice. Despite my personal dislike of Ashbik, I did believe that he had what it took to be emperor.

I strode through the castle as swiftly as I could, putting the politics aside.

I wanted to find her.

HAZEL

I stood against the door to Tejus's room. My flesh was prickling with goosebumps and my heart was racing.

Had I heard correctly? I still couldn't quite believe that I had. Because if I had, that meant that Tejus had just committed an act completely devoid of selfishness. I had waited outside the door of the council chambers, and I had heard his speech. I had heard the sound of a man standing up for what he believed in, against all the odds, against every single instinct that his upbringing had instilled in him.

He had changed.

He had become the man I'd known he could be.

I heard his sure-footed approach from the corridor. He

must have left his ministers to dispute over the outcome without him.

I jumped away from the door. It swung open a second later, and Tejus stood in its frame, looking murderous.

"Why didn't you go to the human quarters like I told you to?" he barked at me.

I smiled at him softly. He could no longer aggravate me with his commands—they were for my safety, and I knew that he prioritized that above most things. Tejus and I still had a lot to learn about each other, but of some things I was sure. Tejus was a good man, and he could say and do things to try to dissuade me and the rest of the world of that fact, but I would no longer be fooled.

And I couldn't stay silent a moment longer. Tejus had to know how I felt—and that I would no longer be accepting his refusal.

I opened my mouth, and tried to speak.

I couldn't.

What? No...not now!

I tried again, watching confusion pass through Tejus's expression. No matter how hard I tried, not a sound would come out.

The pestilence of silence.

Now?!

I could have screamed. *Of all the times the final apocalyptic warning could have picked to show up...* Instead, I watched Tejus try to speak, trying as I had and failing. The rest of the castle had fallen completely silent too—there were no faint mutterings of the ministers, no yells and commands from the servants' quarters, no crying or complaining from the kids in the human quarters. It was like a blanket had been placed over the world, settling it into sleep.

There are other ways to communicate.

I approached Tejus. He stood still, watching me closely. As I got closer, I could see that his heart was pounding, and that every muscle in his body had tensed—as if he was readying himself for battle, to fight off his enemies, to conquer. But there was nothing left for him to fight. Not tonight, anyway.

I took both his hands in mine. He frowned down at me, unsure. I smiled, and pushed out my mind toward his. I saw understanding dawn on his face, and he latched onto the energy that I was offering. Our minds started to entwine, the golden rope appearing, seeming like it was lengthening rather than thickening—and in my mind I saw it start to entwine our bodies together, its glow lighting up our skin and pushing us closer together.

I sent him the memory of standing outside the door,

listening to his speech to the ministers. I pushed my feelings toward him—my love and determination.

I love you, Tejus. Don't refuse me anymore. Please surrender. Give us a chance.

His eyes softened as he looked down toward mine. I no longer had any idea if we were in the mind meld or not. He drew me closer to him, his arms sliding around my waist. Then images started to flicker in my mind.

Oh…wow.

They were his memories. The day I arrived in Nevertide, my face enraged and yelling at him; my fear of jumping over the last stone during the labyrinth trial; holding me after our victory at the disk trial; my face lighting up when he first showed me the library; peering up from the bottom of the temple; the first time he'd seen me in the gown I'd worn to his coronation; smiling at him in the firelight on the night of the ice fires; then our first kiss.

You love me.

His lips met mine, and the memories melted away. I kissed him back, my hands running up his chest. The mind-meld broke. The room—the tapestries, the velvet sofas, the books and swords—all should have come rushing back into focus, but all I saw was Tejus.

I broke the kiss, panting. His eyes held a question, but,

speechless, I had to show him what I wanted. With trembling fingers, I undid the button at the top of his shirt. His hands moved over mine, stilling them.

His expression looked troubled, but I gently removed his hands from mine.

This is what I want.

I moved down to the next button, my movements surer now. I didn't want to give him another excuse to stop me— he *had* to know how I felt, and this was the way I wanted to show him, with my body, with my touch. All of me.

I ran my fingers across his chest, and I felt his breath hitch. The scars were still there, jagged spikes across his smooth, pale skin. I gently eased his shirt backward off his shoulders, exposing his collarbone and fully exposing the broadness of his frame.

You're so beautiful.

Up close, able to touch him in this way, I was awestruck.

His shirt fell away, and I smiled up at him. It dimmed when I saw the hesitation in his eyes—there was reluctance there, and I didn't know why. I never knew why.

Please?

My fingers pressed into the skin on his stomach, and the muscles jumped beneath my touch as he inhaled sharply. He wanted me. Wasn't that enough?

He closed his eyes for a moment, shutting me out. When he reopened them, I could see that he'd come to a conclusion. The pupils grew wider; his eyes became hooded and dark.

Without warning, he picked me up. Afraid to fall, I wrapped my arms around his neck. He moved me to his bedroom, not taking his eyes off me. He shut the door and locked it. He laid me gently down on the bed and knelt on all fours over me.

His hair brushed against my face. I tugged at it gently, pulling his lips down toward mine again. The kiss was hot, needy. It became more and more urgent with every passing second, and my head started to spin in the most amazing way.

This time he broke the kiss, and we both came away breathless and panting. He ran his hand from my hip up to the side of my waist. He looked at me with a questioning expression—was I sure? Was I ready?

I nodded, but he knew already. Gently, with agonizingly slow movements, he removed my pants and shirt, leaving me in my underwear. I felt exposed and too vulnerable, but as his gaze heated, tracing the curves of my body, it no longer seemed to matter.

He bared me completely, tenderly brushing my skin with

his fingers. Then he moved off the bed, standing up and removing his clothes, tossing them carelessly on the floor. I couldn't help but gape.

He climbed back on top of me, holding the back of my neck in one hand and pulling my lips toward him. He kissed my lips, softly, chastely, and then marked me with butterfly kisses from the corner of my mouth, down the nape of my neck. My skin felt like it was on fire.

I could feel the tautness of every muscle in his body, and the tension between his legs. My body started to hum with anticipation—intense, flickering heat that flowered up within me. He smiled up at me from where his kisses had finished, and then re-covered my body with his own.

His tongue explored my mouth, and I felt like I was rolling into oblivion, a heady, shaking kind of heaven. As our bodies molded together as one, I felt a bittersweet pain, and then nothing but wave upon wave of ecstasy. A warm glow spread around our bodies, and I didn't know if it was my imagination or not, but I felt like the golden rope of our mind-melds had reappeared, linking us inextricably together—heart, mind and soul.

Tejus took a shuddering breath, and explored deeper. I clasped him tightly to me. I would never let go. My mind felt as if it was floating off somewhere above me, and the only thing keeping me in this land was being tethered to Tejus—unable to look away from his glittering dark eyes.

You're mine, I thought, hoping that he could hear me. *Always.*

Rose

We were back in The Shade; Corrine and Mona were off gathering a team of witches who were going to help us in our search for a portal. Caleb and I were studying maps, looking for the likeliest co-ordinates from which to begin our search.

"This isn't going to be easy," Caleb murmured. He traced his fingers over the length of the British Isles, all the way down to the rest of Northern Europe.

"It's a lot of area to cover," I agreed. I was starting to worry—how long was it going to take for us to explore the miles of sea?

"I think our best bet will be to split into two teams," Caleb said, "one heading to the North Atlantic, and the other sticking to the North Sea. We can't ignore that area, it's just as viable a location for the portal if we're talking about aviation travel."

Ashley and Landis had reported the same as we had—a few locals noticing weird bird migration patterns in Guernsey, and one old man mentioning seeing extremely large birds in the sky at night that he had sworn were vultures.

"Corrine back yet?" Claudia asked, walking into the room with a box of headsets that we were going to use to communicate while at sea.

"Not yet," I muttered distractedly, studying the maps.

"Well, we need to get a move on." Claudia had become increasingly agitated since returning from Portugal. She and Yuri had come up empty on every lead that they followed, and I could share her frustration—but I didn't want to rush headlong into this. If we picked the wrong ocean spots, then we would seriously delay our investigation.

"I know," Corrine replied tersely, suddenly appearing behind Claudia at the door. "We're moving as fast as we can, but believe me, this isn't going to be easy—and you can't expect instant results, even if the theory is correct."

She was right. There was a big question mark over this theory—and for such an ambitious undertaking, we were placing a lot of faith in the assumption that the birds were connected to the disappearance to our kids, and that they would be coming from the sea somewhere…

"It's the only lead we have. We have to at least try," I told them both.

"So what's the plan?" Corrine asked.

Caleb showed where he'd marked out the likely co-ordinates on the map, and proposed splitting ourselves up to cover more ground.

"How many witches do we have?" Caleb asked.

"Ten, not including Mona and Corrine. It's a good start. Mona will take one team, and I'll head up the other. Although the North Atlantic is going to be the trickiest—there are fewer islands there, and it's obviously much larger. The North Sea has plenty—especially up by Scotland." Corrine studied the map intently. "We'll travel to the Fair Isle in the North Sea, and Île Saint-Nicolas in the Atlantic."

We divided up the teams, Caleb and I going with Corrine and three other witches, and Claudia, Yuri, Ashley and Landis going with Mona and seven other witches as the slightly larger team to take on the North Atlantic.

"The rest of the witches will be here in an hour," Corrine said. "Suit up. Everyone take a headset."

We all returned to our treehouses. After entering our

AN EMPIRE OF STONES

apartment, Caleb and I hurried straight to the bedroom, where we changed into water-resistant uniforms. My entire body felt tense and anxious, and I fumbled with my zipper twice.

"Here," Caleb said, taking over. He ran the zipper up my back, and the familiar feeling of my husband's firm touch restored some of my sanity.

"I'm trying to treat it like any other case," I murmured, "but it's hard. Every time I look at Claudia or any of the other parents, I feel guilty. It was my decision to send the kids to that camp…"

"Don't think like that," Caleb reprimanded me. "How were you to know? None of us could have predicted this."

I knew that he was right, but it didn't stop me from feeling like a pretty crappy mom right now.

"Let's leave," I croaked.

We made our way back to the courtyard outside the Sanctuary, where the witches were waiting for us—along with Claudia and Yuri, and Ashley and Landis. We were ready to go.

* * *

"Anything?" I asked for what felt like the fifteen millionth time.

302

Corrine shook her head wearily, not even bothering to reply. I looked out on the endless ocean, its waters calm for the moment, the sun dancing about on the tops of the placid waves. There was nothing to be seen for miles, just an endless expanse of blue. We had taken a sea plane instead of a boat, hoping that we'd be able to cover more ground, but it hadn't made much difference. We had to go slowly so the witches could get a sense of what was going on in the water, and then we paused every so often to refuel from the massive storage tank that we carried.

At each side of the plane, witches stood at the open doors, scanning the water—seeing if they could pick up on any surges or disruption that might indicate that a portal was close by.

"Claudia?" I called into my headset. "Anything?"

The line was really bad at such a long distance, but after a few seconds' delay, she came in.

"Nothing. Not yet."

Ugh. "Okay."

I switched it off, and sighed. Caleb gave my knee a squeeze.

"We knew this would take some time," he said.

I leaned back, trying to think positively, when the muttering of two witches made me look over to the right side of the plane. Corrine hastened over from her side, and they started talking animatedly. I looked at Caleb, hardly daring to hope…

"Corrine?"

She turned around, beckoning me to the side of the plane.

"Look at this!" she exclaimed.

Caleb and I rushed over to her, leaning out to look at the water. Up ahead we saw the waters rushing and swirling — creating huge ripples on the surface of the water and massive white-foam sprays that flew up noisily, and which were starting to affect the drift of the plane.

"Let's get closer!"

We had taken one of the younger GASP members to man the plane, and he nodded, accelerating over to the source of the activity.

We flew higher, avoiding the now large waves that were being created by the swirl up ahead.

"I'm definitely getting something," murmured one of the witches, her eyes closed as she tried to focus on the energy.

"It's a portal," Corrine acknowledged with a smile. "I can sense it."

We passed right over the swirl. Looking down, we saw what looked like a small typhoon in the water—the ocean swirled downward for about a mile until a black disk hovered in the center of the swirl. It wasn't like most of the portals I'd ever seen—that normally seemed to hint at another world behind it, like a galaxy of stars or blue skies. This surface was as thick as black tar, moving slowly and sluggishly as if it was alive.

"Oh, my God," I croaked, clasping Caleb's hand.

"We found it," he breathed.

All of us stared, speechless, at the hole in the ocean beneath us.

SHERUS

It started with a pain. As if a rock-hard hand was clutching at my heart, tightening its grip, making me want to scream out.

I sat up in bed, my fingers pressing against my chest, trying to calm the sensation. It was the middle of the night, and my chamber was empty, the red glows of bloodstone providing the only light. I looked around wildly, a sixth sense picking up on some strangeness that I couldn't define, but all the same, it was enough to make the hairs on the back of my neck stand on end.

The pain in my heart receded, and gingerly I stepped out of my bed. Leaving the warmth of the covers behind, I stood shivering in the middle of the room, my gaze drawn to the draped windows that were fluttering gently in the breeze.

There was nothing wrong here—why did I feel like there was?

I walked over to the windows, pulling back the drapes. To my relief, the night sky was as it always was: the fae planets shining brightly up ahead, filling me with comfort. I watched for a while, until I heard the pitter-patter of summer rains emerging from the sky. Getting cold, I was about to turn away from the window and return to my dreams when a violent tear of lightning ripped through the sky.

I watched in horror as the prongs of light appeared to split up the fae planets—a sharp dagger of yellowing light appearing in the space between each of them, as if the very universe was being split.

So it has come to pass.

The evil had awoken.

I staggered back from the window, unable to tear my eyes away from the night sky. It was a few moments till I recovered my wits. As soon as I did, I called for my guards until my throat was dry.

Hazel

Wow.

Oh, wow.

I lay entwined in the mussed-up sheets of Tejus's bed, our limbs touching lightly—my foot resting against his calf, his arm falling above my head, my hair brushing up against the side of his body. Tejus was lying on his back, his breath rising and falling deeply in sleep.

I smiled up at the ceiling.

I didn't want this moment to end; I didn't want the rest of the night to come, and I rejected the idea of dawn bringing realities to be faced and fought. What we had shared had been perfect—mind-blowing, like my insides had been turned upside down and every cell in my body had been transformed and linked with his. I'd had no idea that it would be like this. Was it because he was a sentry and had a unique tunnel into my head, into every emotion and sensation I was feeling? Or was it like this for everybody?

No way.

I smirked. Everyone would be walking around floating on clouds if it was. Tejus had made my world stop turning, had completely obliterated my mind until there had been nothing left but soft, silent sighs of bliss.

Gently, careful not to wake him, I turned on my side to face him. I could hardly believe it had happened—that he had finally surrendered, in the best possible way. Reaching out my hand, I placed it softly on his chest, wanting to feel the ropes of muscle, the rough skin of his scars, and the slow beat of his heart.

Tejus's skin flickered at my touch, and his eyes opened. He looked down at me with a soft expression. He raised an eyebrow and I smiled guiltily.

Busted.

I went to remove my hand, but his came over mine, holding it in place. I smiled, feeling a strange, but not unpleasant sensation fluttering through my skull. It grew stronger, becoming heady and invigorating.

It took me a split second to realize what was happening, and I looked up at Tejus in confusion. Was he trying to mind-meld with me?

His expression suggested otherwise.

He looked horrified.

What?

I moved my hand away abruptly, holding it to my own chest as if I needed to forcefully stop it returning to his. The flickers in my mind were growing stronger, like electricity was accumulating in my brain. As shocked and weirded-out as I was, I didn't want the feeling to stop…

More.

I need more.

I drew the sheets around me, backing away from the bed. Tejus was sitting up, his heart visibly racing, a sheen of perspiration appearing across his forehead. I stumbled on the sheets, holding onto the bed frame to steady myself.

I paused, watching Tejus. I couldn't seem to escape the sudden, overwhelming feeling of hunger. *Real* hunger—as if I'd never really felt the sensation before; what I'd previously assumed was hunger now just seemed like a shadow of this feeling. It was raw, exposed, like I had a huge, gaping hole in my soul and I could only satisfy it with whatever Tejus had given me…

Energy.

My eyes widened.

I just syphoned off Tejus.

The shock should have been enough for me to come to my senses. It wasn't. I could only focus on the fact that I wanted more...surely he had enough to share with me?

He's wounded! I screamed at myself. *You can't!*

But I was so hungry...I took a few steps closer, every part of me lusting for his energy—it was so potent, so powerful. It was like a pure elixir flowed through Tejus's veins, the one thing in this world that would satisfy me.

What is happening to you?!

Tejus was slowly backing up against the end of the bed as if he was in the room with a wild animal. His eyes were still horrified, his face deathly pale, as if his worst nightmare was taking place before him.

Our eyes met; whatever spell I had been under broke abruptly. I felt like someone had just thrown a bucket of cold water over me as a horrific clarity sharpened the scene in front of me. I clutched the bed frame, gasping.

How is this even possible?

I opened my mouth to scream, feeling like my lungs were ripping apart even though no sound escaped.

Have I just become... a sentry?

READY FOR THE NEXT PART OF THE NOVAK CLAN'S STORY?

Dear Shaddict,

Thank you for continuing the adventure with me!

You'll be glad to know that you don't have to wait long for the next book. _ASOV 38: A Power of Old_, releases <u>January 9th, 2017</u>. (My first release of 2017!)

Pre-order your copy now and have it delivered automatically to your reading device on release day.

Visit: <u>www.bellaforrest.net</u> for details.

I'll see you back in The Shade in the new year. Happy holidays!

Love,
Bella xxx

P.S. Join my VIP email list and I'll send you a personal reminder as soon as I have a new book out. Visit here to sign up: **www.forrestbooks.com**

(You'll also be the first to receive news about movies/TV show as well as other exciting projects that may be coming up!)

P.P.S. Follow The Shade on Instagram and check out some of the beautiful graphics: @ashadeofvampire

You can also come say hi on Facebook:
www.facebook.com/AShadeOfVampire
And Twitter: @ashadeofvampire

Made in the USA
San Bernardino, CA
28 May 2017